THE LIFE OF
LAZARILLO DE TORMES

A Digireads.com Book
Digireads.com Publishing

Lazarillo de Tormes
By Anonymous
Translated by Clements Markham
ISBN: 1-4209-3428-7

Please visit *www.digireads.com*

The Life

of

Lazarillo de Tormes

His Fortunes & Adversities

TRANSLATED FROM THE EDITION OF 1554

(PRINTED AT BURGOS)

BY

SIR CLEMENTS MARKHAM, K.C.B.

D.Sc. (CAMB.)

WITH A NOTICE OF THE MENDOZA FAMILY,
A SHORT LIFE OF THE AUTHOR, DON DIEGO
HURTADO DE MENDOZA, A NOTICE OF
THE WORK, AND SOME REMARKS ON THE
CHARACTER OF LAZARILLO DE TORMES

Lazarillo begging.

ANALYTICAL TABLE OF CONTENTS

INTRODUCTORY

THE FAMILY OF MENDOZA

DON DIEGO HURTADO DE MENDOZA, AUTHOR OF "LAZARILLO DE TORMES"

THE BOOK, "LAZARILLO DE TORMES"

ix

TABLE OF CONTENTS

TABLE OF CONTENTS

SECOND MASTER

HOW LAZARO TOOK SERVICE WITH A CLERGYMAN, AND OF THE THINGS THAT HAPPENED TO HIM

THIRD MASTER

HOW LAZARO TOOK SERVICE WITH A GENTLEMAN, AND WHAT HAPPENED TO HIM

TABLE OF CONTENTS

FOURTH MASTER

HOW LAZARO TOOK SERVICE WITH A FRIAR OF THE ORDER OF MERCY, AND WHAT HAPPENED TO HIM

TABLE OF CONTENTS

FIFTH MASTER

HOW LAZARO TOOK SERVICE WITH A SELLER OF PAPAL INDULGENCES

SIXTH MASTER

HOW LAZARO TOOK SERVICE WITH A CHAPLAIN, AND HOW HE PROSPERED

SEVENTH MASTER

HOW LAZARO TOOK SERVICE WITH A CONSTABLE, AND WHAT HAPPENED AFTERWARDS

LIST OF ILLUSTRATIONS

BY STEPHEN BAGHOT DE LA BERE

Sketch Map of Route at end of Volume.

INTRODUCTORY

THE FAMILY OF MENDOZA

THE author of *Lazarillo de Tormes* was a scion of one of the noblest families of Spain, and some account of it Descent of the author of *Lazarillo de Tormes*. should precede a notice of the author's life.[1]

Don Diego Lopez, Lord of Mendoza, in 1170 married Doña Eleanor Hurtado, heiress of Mendibil. She was the daughter of Fernan Perez de Lara called Hurtado, son of Pedro Gonzalez de Lara and of the Queen Urraca of Castille and Leon.

Don Lopez and Eleanor Hurtado had four sons : Inigo, Lord of Mendoza ; Diego, Lord of Mendibil ; Pedro Diaz, who was ancestor of the Mendozas of Seville ; and Fernando, who founded the line in Portugal.

Inigo Lopez de Mendoza married Maria de Haro, and was father of Maria, the wife of her first cousin, Juan de Mendoza, son of her

---

[1] Doubt has been thrown on the authorship, but without sufficient reason. See Antonio, *Bib. Nov.* i. 291.

uncle Diego. Their son, Diego Hurtado de Mendoza, in the time of Fernando II., married Maria Gonzalez de Aguero, and had a son Gonzalo.

This Gonzalo Hurtado de Mendoza married Juana Fernandez de Orozco, and was the father of a very distinguished son—of Pedro Gonzalez.

Pedro Gonzalez Hurtado de Mendoza married Aldonza, daughter of Fernan Perez de Ayala. He was with Juan I., of Castille, at the battle of Alju-barrota. In the flight the King's horse was killed. Mendoza dismounted and said to the King :—

> A Mendoza saved the life of King Juan I. of Castille.

> El cavallo vos han muerto,[1]
> Subid Rey en mi cavallo.

The King rode away. Mendoza was over-taken and slain. The date of the battle was August 14, 1385. His father survived him, dying in 1405.

The son of this chivalrous knight and successor to his grandfather was Diego Hurtado de Mendoza, married first to Maria, daughter of Enrique II., King of Castille, and secondly to Eleanor de la Vega. His son, Inigo Lopez, was by his second wife.

[1] They have killed the horse of thine,
Save *thy* life and mount on mine.

THE FAMILY OF MENDOZA

Inigo Lopez Hurtado de Mendoza was born in 1396. He served with distinction at the battle of Olmedo, and was created Marquis of Santillana in 1445. He was opposed to Alvaro de Luna, the famous Minister of Juan II.

The Poet Marquis of Santillana.

Born in the Asturias, the Marquis was a poet. Among his writings was a little *Serranilla*.

Moza tan fermosa
No vi en la frontera
Como una vaquera
De la Finojosa.

En un verde prado
De rosas y flores
Guardando ganado
Con otras pastores.

La vi tan fermosa
Que apenas creyera
Que fuese vaquera
De la Finojosa.

TRANSLATION

The sweetest girl without compare
In all my days I've ever seen
Was that young maid, so lithe and fair,
On Finojosa's frontier green.

In pleasant shade of beech and pine
A verdant meadow did appear ;
And here she watched the browsing kine
With other girls, but none like her.

INTRODUCTORY

By nature deck'd and well arrayed
She looked like some bright Summer Queen ;
And not a common village maid
Of Finojosa's frontier green.

But the chief poetical work of the Marquis of Santillana was the *Comedieta de Ponza*, founded on the story of a great sea-fight, near the island of Ponza, in 1435, between the Aragon fleet and the Genoese. At the request of King Juan II. he also made a *collection of proverbs* for his son Enrique IV. This was the earliest collection of proverbs made in modern times.

The noble poet married Catalina Suarez _{Children of the Marquis of Santillana.} de Figueroa, daughter of Don Lorenzo Suarez de Figueroa, Lord of Feria and Zafra. The Marquis died in 1454, leaving ten children :—

1. Don Diego Hurtado de Mendoza, first Duke of Infantado.

2. Don Pedro Laso de Mendoza, married to Anes Carillo, Lady of Mondejar. They had two daughters :—

    1. Maria, married to the second Count of Tendilla.

    2. Catalina, married to Luis de la Cerda, Duke of Medina Celi.

3. Don Inigo Lopez de Mendoza, first Count of Tendilla, of whom we treat.

4. Don Lorenzo de Mendoza, first Count of Coruña.
5. Don Pedro Gonzalez de Mendoza, Archbishop of Toledo and Cardinal.
6. Don Juan de Mendoza, Lord of Colmenar.
7. Don Pedro de Mendoza, Lord of Sazedon.
8. Doña Mencia, wife of Don Pedro de Velasco, Count of Haro, Constable of Spain.
9. Doña Maria, married to Don Ajan de Ribero.
10. Doña Eleanor, wife of Gaston de la Cerda, second Count of Medina Celi, representative of the eldest son of Alfonso X. and therefore rightful King of Spain ; the reigning family descending from the second son, the usurper Sancho.

Don Inigo Lopez de Mendoza was created first Count of Tendilla in 1465. He was Captain-General of Andalusia. He married Doña Elvira de Quiñones, daughter of Don Diego Fernandez, Lord of Luna. Their children were :— The Counts of Tendilla.

1. Don Inigo Lopez de Mendoza, second Count of Tendilla.
2. Don Diego de Mendoza, Archbishop of Seville.

3. Don Pedro de Mendoza, married to Juana Nuñez Cabeza de Vaca.

4. Doña Catalina, wife of Don Diego de Sandoval, Marquis of Denia.

5. Doña Mencia, wife of Don Pedro Carillo, Lord of Toralva.

Don Inigo Lopez de Mendoza, second Count of Tendilla and first Marquis of Mondejar, Grandee of Spain and Viceroy of Granada. He married his first cousin, Doña Maria Laso de Mendoza, but had no children by her. He married, secondly, Doña Francisca Pacheco, daughter of the Duke of Escalona, by whom he had eight children :—

1. Don Luis de Mendoza, third Count of Tendilla, Viceroy of Navarre, President of the Council of the Indies, second Marquis of Mondejar, Captain-General of Granada.

2. Don Bernardo de Mendoza, slain at St. Quentin, 1557.

3. Don Antonio de Mendoza, Viceroy of Peru, 1550.

4. Don Francisco de Mendoza, Bishop of Jaen.

5. Don Diego Hurtado de Mendoza, of whom we treat.

THE FAMILY OF MENDOZA

6. Don Bernardino de Mendoza, General of the galleys.

7. Doña Maria de Mendoza, wife of the Count of Monteagudo.

8. Doña Maria Pacheco, married to Don Juan de Padilla.

> Veinte y tres generaciones
> La prosapia de Mendoza
> No hay linage en toda España
> De quien conozca
> Tan notable antiguedad.
>
> LOPE DE VEGA.

DON DIEGO HURTADO DE MENDOZA, AUTHOR OF "LAZARILLO DE TORMES"

Don Diego Hurtado de Mendoza was the fifth son of the Marquis of Mondejar and Count of Tendilla, first Spanish Governor of Granada, by Francisca Pacheco, daughter of the Duke of Escalona.

The Governor had a palace in the Alhambra near the Torre de Picos, which is now demolished. But the smaller house of his esquire, Antasio de Bracamonte, still stands in a garden, built against the exquisite little mosque on the walls. There are three shields of arms carved on the walls of Bracamonte's house.

The palace and the esquire's house, both within the walls of the Alhambra, looked across the valley of the Darro to the Albacain. Both buildings were surrounded by gardens and fruit-trees. In this romantic spot Diego was born in the year 1503, and he passed his early years with his brothers and sisters there. Pedro

Birth of Don Diego in the Alhambra.

Martir de Angleria was his tutor. At an early age he went to the university of Salamanca, where he learnt Latin, Greek, and Arabic, and studied canon and civil law.

While he was a student at Salamanca Don Diego wrote *Lazarillo de Tormes.*

Don Diego at Salamanca.

On leaving the university Don Diego went to serve with the Spanish armies in Italy. He also attended lectures at Rome, Bologna, and Padua, and was a profound scholar as well as a statesman and a soldier. Charles V. appreciated his ability and his acquirements. In 1538, at the age of thirty-five, he was appointed Ambassador at Venice. He assisted and patronised the Aldi, and Josephus was first printed complete from his library. Afterwards he was for some time Military Governor of Sienna; and he was sent to the Council of Trent to maintain the imperial interests there. His next employment was at Rome, as special Plenipotentiary to rebuke and overawe Pope Julius III., which he did.

His services in Italy.

Don Diego Hurtado de Mendoza returned to Spain in 1554 at the age of fifty. He was not appreciated by Philip II. and seldom came to Court, living,

The library.

with his splendid library, in his house at Granada.

In his retirement he wrote a good deal of poetry. But his great work was the *Guerra de Granada*, a narrative of the *The Guerra de Granada.* rebellion of the Moors in 1568-1570. He did the Moors such impartial justice that his book could not be published until many years after his death. Sallust was his model. The first edition appeared in 1610, and the second more complete edition at Valencia in 1776. It is one of the finest pieces of prose - writing in the Spanish language.

In his last years Don Diego found much pleasant employment in his library. He corresponded with Zurita, the *Last days.* historian of Aragon, telling him how the work of looking over his books reminded him of many long-forgotten things, and supplied him with much food for thought. While in Italy he had been diligent in obtaining Greek MSS., and in other respects his library was quite unique. He bequeathed it to Philip II., and it is now in the Escurial.

Don Diego died at Madrid in *Death of Don Diego Hurtado de Mendoza.* April 1575, aged 72.

THE BOOK

TICKNOR [1] describes *Lazarillo de Tormes* as "a work of genius unlike anything that had preceded it. Its object is to give a pungent satire on all classes of society. It is written in a very bold, rich, and idiomatic Castilian style. Some of its sketches are among the most fresh and spirited that can be found in the whole range of prose works of fiction. Those of the friar and the seller of Indulgences were put under the ban of the Church." They were expurgated by the Inquisition in 1573, when an expurgated edition was published at Madrid, and in the *Index Expurgatorius* of 1667.

Ticknor's opinion of the work.

The first edition in Spain was published at Burgos in 1554.[2] It is excessively rare. There is a copy at Chatsworth, but none in the British Museum. The Duke of Devonshire allowed the late Mr. H. Butler

First edition.

[1] *History of Spanish Literature*, i. 469-71.
[2] Brunet mentions an Antwerp edition of 1553.

Clarke to transcribe his copy of the first edition. This was done with great care, exactly as it was printed. In 1897 Mr. Butler Clarke printed 250 copies at Oxford, with a facsimile of the old title-page.

Many other editions followed the first of 1554.[1] In Mr. Grenville's library there is an Value of copies. Antwerp edition (12mo) of 1555, for which he paid seven guineas. Colonel Stanley's copy fetched £31 : 10s. ; Mr. Hanroth's, £20 : 10s. The Paris editor of 1827 could only find a 1595 edition.

A second part, by some wretched scribbler, soon appeared, without any merit. It makes Spurious second parts. Lazarillo go to sea in the Algiers expedition of 1541. The ship founders, he sinks to the bottom, crawls into a cave, and is turned into a tunny fish. He is then caught in a seine, returns by an effort of will to the human form, and finally goes to live at Salamanca. There was another second part by Juan de Luna, a teacher of Spanish at Paris. It continues the story by making Lazaro serve several other masters, and then become a religious recluse. Both second parts

---

[1] At Tarragona, 1586 ; Zaragoza, 1595 ; Medina del Campo and Valladolid, 1603 ; Zaragoza again, 1652, with Luna's second part ; Madrid, 1664, without the second part. There was a new edition published at Paris in 1847, with the second parts.

are miserable rubbish, and ought never to be reprinted.

Yet they are included in recent Spanish editions, which is much to be deplored. For the work itself is a classic. In at least two instances the Dictionary of the Spanish Academy refers to *Lazarillo de Tormes* as an authority for the meaning of words.

ENGLISH TRANSLATIONS

Lazarillo de Tormes was first translated into English by David Rowlands of Anglesey. He called it *The Pleasant History of Lazarillo de Tormes drawn out of Spanish.* It was published by Abel Jeffes in the Fore Street without Grepell-gate near Groube Street at the sign of the Bell, and dedicated to Sir Thomas Gresham. It contains the Prologue, and a short chapter at the end about Lazaro's continued prosperity, which is not in the first edition of 1554. This is the best translation. It was published in 1586.

A new edition appeared in 1596, also published by Abel Jeffes, who had then removed to the Blacke Fryers near Puddle Wharfe. There were twenty editions or reprints, and *Lazarillo* was exceedingly popular with the Elizabethan reading public.

ENGLISH TRANSLATIONS

James Blakiston brought out a new edition in 1653 dedicated to Lord Chandos. It consists of the translation by David Rowlands, omitting the Prologue, and of a translation of the spurious second part by Juan de Luna. Another edition appeared in 1669, another in 1677. The title is *The Excellent History of Lazarillo de Tormes, the witty Spaniard.*

In 1726 there appeared *The Life and Adventures of Lazarillo de Tormes, with twenty curious copper cuts.* In 1727 the nineteenth edition was published. This version is a bad translation, omits the Prologue, and includes the spurious second parts.

The worst performance of all was the edition of 1789 in two volumes. The type is better, but it is a very careless reprint of a bad translation. It omits the execrable illustrations of the earlier editions. Spanish names are scarcely recognisable. Gelves is called " the battle of Geleas ! " for Escalona we have " Evealona."

All these translations are from late editions ; none from the first edition.

NOTES ON THE CHARACTER
OF LAZARO

THE conception of the author, Don Diego Hurtado de Mendoza, was first to portray a boy, with everything against him, rising from the lowest rank of society to a prosperous condition, and to give a humorous account of his adventures ; and secondly, to satirise certain types of men, the products of the age in which he wrote, through the medium of his boy hero.

The author himself was a boy at the time, or at least a very young man, a student at Salamanca. He had no model, and the conception was quite original. He makes Lazarillo de Tormes a boy of his own age. Don Diego was born in 1503. Assuming Lazarillo to have been born in 1503,[1] he was about 10 years old when he took service with the blind man, three years

The author made Lazaro's age coincide with his own.

---

[1] Lazarillo was about eight years old when his father went in the Gelves expedition in 1510.

with his first three masters, and 14 years old when he took service with the seller of Indulgences. He carried on the business of water-carrier from the ages of 15 to 19, and was 20 when he married. That would bring him to 1523. The next year, when the Cortes met at Toledo, is made to be the year when Lazarillo de Tormes wrote the story of his life. Doubtless it was the year when Don Diego really completed his little romance, also aged 21.

In conceiving the character of Lazaro it is likely that the young student had in his mind *The author's conception of the two destinies.* what he himself might have been, if he had been born in the same obscurity. "The two destinies"[1] were framed out of a noble and an ignoble birth, success in the latter case being far more meritorious than in the former. We find this reflection in the last sentence of the Prologue, where Don Diego points out how much more those have done who, not being favoured by noble birth, have, nevertheless, by cleverness and force of character, arrived at a good estate. If this idea of a boy such as the author, but without his noble birth and other advantages, was in Don Diego's mind, we should expect to find Lazaro portrayed as a boy of a naturally good disposition and fine instincts, whose bad

[1] See Sir Francis Doyle's poem.

qualities were due to his lowly birth and
vicious surroundings. It is just such a boy
as this that Don Diego presents to us.

Nothing could be worse than poor Lazaro's
home. His mother was a widow who had
intimacies with a groom of Moorish _{Lazaro's baneful}
blood, had a child by him, and lived _{surroundings}
_{as a child.}
on the proceeds of his thieving, _{His mother not}
while Lazaro was employed to dis- _{unfeeling.}
pose of the stolen goods. When they were
found out, the widow's position became most
precarious. Just then the wonderfully clever
and plausible blind man appeared on the scene.
He offered what, in comparison with the boy's
lot with his mother, seemed to be a decent
provision. She is accused of unfeeling conduct
in thus parting with her son. I do not think
this is intended. The poor woman did what
she thought was best for the child, and their
parting was sorrowful and affectionate. Don
Diego made her a thief and worse, but not a
mother without feeling.

The account of the professional cleverness
and knowledge of the blind man is very
interesting, but, in spite of it all, the _{Capital stories}
little boy seems to have held his own _{most amusingly}
_{told.}
to some extent with the old rascal.
The trick with the half blancas, the story of
the wine, and of the bunch of grapes, are

capitally told and very amusing. It is true that the old man was handicapped by his blindness, though his strength, cleverness, and experience made up for it. He treated Lazaro abominably, but it must be acknowledged that, great as the provocation was, the boy's revenge was cruel and unfeeling. He was sorry afterwards, for he wrote that his understanding was blinded in that hour.

The boy's ingenious ways of getting at the provisions of his second master, who was starving him, are capitally and most amusingly told. But the funniest and most witty story in the book is the boy's terror at the coffin he believed to be coming to the house, and the reason he thought so.

With the first two masters it was an incessant fight against starvation. Lazaro's resourceful ingenuity was conspicuous, and, under the circumstances, he had a perfect right to use all his wits against the wretches who ill-treated him. But there was no opportunity of bringing out his finer qualities.

With the third master it was very different. He was a penniless esquire, starving himself, and so excessively proud that he thought only of concealing his poverty. Lazaro had to resort to begging, and so he kept his poor master, as well as himself, alive.

OF THE CHARACTER

Here Lazaro comes out in an excellent light. He was not only kind-hearted and generous, but he showed tact and a wish to Lazaro's higher avoid hurting the poor proud qualities shown in his inter- creature's feelings. Don Diego thus course with the shows his hero in the light of one esquire. of nature's gentlemen. The esquire's account of himself, and his views of honour and its obligations are interesting, as showing a type of character which was common in Spain in those days. It was more elaborately portrayed by Cervantes.

Lazaro is made to tell the story of the seller of Indulgences, and a very amusing story it is, no doubt true to life. For it aroused the anger of the Inquisition, and was expurgated from future editions. But Lazaro merely appears as a narrator; and his character is not developed; though it is in the rapid sketch of his rise to prosperity. He was a lad who was Development liked. His girl-friends who were of Lazaro's kind to him in adversity, as well as character. the archpriest and many others who were good friends when he rose to prosperity, showed that he was a favourite among those with whom he came in contact.

His marriage brought him great advantages. Critics have called it disgraceful, because we are told that evil tongues suggested that the girl had been the archpriest's mistress. But there is nothing in the narrative to justify the belief that the evil tongues did not lie. On the contrary, the conclusion is the other way, and the story ends with a defence of his wife by Lazaro himself.

The work is the production of a genius. Its originality, and the admirable way in which the Merits of the stories in it are told make it deserving work. of a wider audience, though of course it is well known to students of the literature of Europe. Seldom has so much wit, fun, and wisdom been gathered into so small a compass.

PROLOGUE

I HOLD it to be good that such remarkable things as have happened to me, perhaps never before seen or heard of, should not Reasons for relating all the circumstances of his life. be buried in the tomb of oblivion. It may be that some one who reads may find something that pleases him. For those who do not go very deep into the matter there is a saying of Pliny "*that there is no book so bad that it does not contain something that is good.*"[1] Moreover, all tastes are not the same, and what one does not eat another will. Thus we see things that are thought much of by some, depreciated by others. Hence no circumstance ought to be omitted, how insignificant soever it may be, but all should be made known, especially as some fruit might be plucked from such a tree.

If this were not so, very few would write

---

[1] Cervantes knew his *Lazarillo* well. He copies this quotation and puts it into the mouth of the curate when he was examining the books of Don Quixote.

at all, for it cannot be done without hard work.

Authors do not wish to be recompensed with money, but by seeing that their work is known and read, and, if it contains anything that is worthy, that it is praised. On this point Tully says : " Honour creates the arts." Think you that the soldier who is first on the ladder cares less for his life than the others? Certainly not. It is the desire for fame that leads him to seek such danger. It is the same in the arts and in letters. We say : " The Doctor preaches very well and he is one who desires much the welfare of souls," but ask him whether he is much offended when they say, " How wonderfully your reverence has done it !" So also in arms, men report how such an one has jousted wretchedly, and he has given his arms to a jester because he praised him for using his lances so well. What would he have given if he had been told the truth? Now that all things go in this manner, I confess that I am not more righteous than my neighbours. I write in this rough style, and all who may find any pleasure in it will be satisfied to know that there lives a man who has met with such fortunes, encountered such dangers, and suffered such adversities. I beseech your

Motives of authors not to gain money, but to win fame.

Honour that you will accept the poor service of one who would be richer if his power was equal to his desire. Well, your Honour! This author writes what he writes, and relates his story very fully.

It seemed to him that he should not begin in the middle, but quite at the beginning, so that there might be a full notice of his personality, and also that those who inherit noble estates may consider how little *Success of the poor should be a lesson to the rich.* fortune owes them, having been so very partial to them in its gifts; and how much more those have done who, not being so favoured, have, by force and management, arrived at a good estate.

PARENTAGE OF LAZARO AND THE REASON FOR HIS SURNAME

I

LAZARO RELATES THE WAY OF HIS BIRTH AND TELLS WHOSE SON HE IS

WELL! your Honour must know, before anything else, that they call me Lazarillo de Tormes, and that I am the son of Thome Gonçales and Antonia Perez, natives of Tejares,[1] a village near Salamanca. My birth was in the river Tormes,[2] for which reason I

---

[1] Tejares is a small village on the left bank of the river Tormes, about two miles from Salamanca. It consists of a church dedicated to San Pedro, and about fifty houses on the skirts of a hill.

[2] The river Tormes rises in the Sierra de Gredos, a range of hills dividing Estremadura from Old Castille, on the confines of the province of Avila. Its chief sources are a large sheet of water called the "Laguna de Gredos," and a perennial stream called "Tornella." Receiving several streams from the Gredos hills, the Tormes flows north, passing by Alba de Tormes, where there is a stone bridge; and then turns north-west, passing Salamanca, where there is another fine stone bridge, and Ledesma. Finally, it falls into the Douro, on the Portuguese frontier. The Tormes turns many flour mills.

have the river for a surname, and it was in this manner.

My father, whom God pardon, had charge of a flour mill which was on the banks of that river. He was the miller there for over fifteen years, and my mother, being one night taken with me in the mill, she gave birth to me there. So that I may say with truth that I was born in the river.

When I was a child of eight years old, they accused my father of certain misdeeds done to the sacks of those who came to have their corn ground. He was taken into custody, and confessed and denied not, suffering persecution for justice's sake. So I trust in God that he is in glory, for the Evangelist tells us that such are blessed. At that time there was a certain expedition against the Moors[1] and among the adventurers was my

---

[1] This expedition against the Moors started from Malaga under the command of Don Garcia de Toledo in 1510, when Lazarillo was seven years old. The fleet first touched at Sicily and then made for the island of Los Gelves, off the African coast, between Tunis and Tripoli, now called Zerbi. With Toledo were Diego de Vera and Count Pedro Navarro. Zerbi was a low sandy island covered with palm-trees, ruled by a Sheikh of its own. The army landed on the 8th of August 1510. But the Spaniards fell into an ambuscade and were defeated, Toledo being among the slain. Four thousand were killed or taken prisoners. The rest escaped to the ships and returned to Sicily. Toledo was a grandson of the first Duke of Alva.

father, who was banished for the affair already mentioned. He went in the position of attendant on a knight who also went, and, with his master, like a loyal servant, he ended his life.

My widowed mother, finding herself without husband or home, determined to betake herself to the good things so as to be among them ; so she went to live in the city. She hired a small house, and was employed to prepare victuals for certain students. She also washed the clothes of the stable-boys who had charge of the horses of the Comendador de la Magdalena.[1] Thus she frequented the stables, she and a dark-coloured man, who was one of those who had the care of the horses. They came to know each other. Sometimes he came to our house late, and went away in the morning. At other times he came to the door in the day-time, with the excuse that he wanted to buy eggs, and walked into the house. At first I did not like him, for I was afraid of his colour and

Death of Lazaro's father, and his mother goes into service.

Flitting.

A swarthy stepfather and a little brown brother.

---

[1] Comendadores were knights of the Orders of Santiago, Calatrava, and Alcantara. Each had a title affixed to their knighthood. The Comendador of La Magdalena was a knight of the Order of Alcantara.

his ugly face. But when I saw that his coming was the sign of better living, I began to like him, for he always brought pieces of meat, bread, and in the winter, fuel to warm us.

This intercourse went on until one day my mother gave me a pretty little brown brother, whom I played with and helped to keep warm. I remember once that when my stepfather was fondling the child, it noticed that my mother and I were white, and that he was not. It frightened the child, who ran to my mother, pointing with its finger and saying, "Mother, he is ugly!" To this he replied laughing; but I noticed the words of my little brother, and, though so young, I said to myself, "How many there are in the world who run from others because they do not see themselves in them."

It was our fate that the intimacy of the Zayde, for so they called my stepfather, came to the ears of the steward. On looking into the matter he found that half the corn he gave out for the horses was stolen, also that the fuel, aprons, pillions, horse-cloths, and blankets were missing, and that when nothing else was left, the horse-shoes were taken. With all this my mother was helped to bring up the

The punishment for receiving and living on stolen goods.

7

child. We need not wonder at a priest or a friar, when one robs the poor, and the other his female devotees to help a friend such as himself, when the love of a poor stable-lad brings him to this.

All I have related was proved, because they cross-questioned me with threats, and being a *Stolen* child I answered and let out all I *horse-shoes.* knew from fear, down to certain horse-shoes which, by my mother's order, I sold to a blacksmith. They flogged my unhappy stepfather, and put my mother on the accustomed penance as a punishment. An order was given that she was not to enter the stables of the Comendador, nor to receive the flogged Zayde in her house.

The poor woman complied with the sentence that she might not lose all; and to *Lazaro helps* avoid danger and silence evil tongues *at the inn.* she went away into service. She *Takes service* *with a blind* was employed in the open gallery *man.* of an inn, and so she contrived to rear the little brother, though suffering from many difficulties. She raised him until he could walk, and me until I was a fine little boy, who went for wine and lights for the guests, and for anything else they wanted.

Lazarillo helps at the Inn.

FIRST MASTER

HOW LAZARO TOOK SERVICE WITH A
BLIND MAN

AT that time a blind man came to lodge at the inn, who, seeing that I would do to lead him, asked for me from my mother. She gave me to him, say- ing that I was the son of a good father, and boasting that he had been killed at the Island of Gelves.[1] She told the blind man that she trusted in God that I would not turn out a worse man than my father, and she begged him to treat me well and look after me, as I was an orphan. He answered that he would do so, and that he received me not as his servant but as his son. Thus it was that I began to serve and to lead my new master. We were in Salamanca for some days, but, as the earnings were not to my master's liking, he determined to go somewhere else. When we were about to depart, I went to see my mother, and, both weeping, she gave me her

Lazaro enters the service of a blind man.

[1] See note, p. 5.

blessing and said, " I shall see you no more.

Lazaro's fare-
well to his
mother.
Strive to be good, and may God direct your ways. You have been brought up, and are now put with a good master. Farewell ! " And so I went away to my master who was waiting for me.

We went out of Salamanca and came to the bridge. There is, at the entrance of it,

A cruel trick
of the wicked
old blind man.
an animal of stone[1] which almost has the shape of a bull. The blind man told me to go near this animal, and, being there, he said, " Lazaro, put your ear against this bull, and you will hear a great noise inside." I did so, like a simpleton, believing it to be as he said. When he felt that my head was against the stone, he raised his hand and gave me a tremendous blow against the devil of a bull, so that I felt

Lazaro and
the blind man.
the pain for more than three days. Then he said to me, " This will teach you that a blind man's boy ought to be one point more knowing than the devil him- self" ; and he laughed heartily at his joke. It seemed to me that, in an instant, I awoke from

---

[1] There was a huge mass of granite rudely carved in the shape of an animal, which had been on the bridge from time im- memorial ; and which Lazarillo thought was like a bull. Its great weight was considered a danger, and it was removed about thirty years ago. It is now in the vestibule of the cloister of San Domingo at Salamanca, but without a head.

" He answered that he received me, not as his servant but as his son."

my simplicity in which I had reposed from childhood. I said to myself, "This man says truly that it behoves me to keep my eyes open, for I am alone and have to think for myself."

We set out on our road, and in a very few days I showed myself to be sprightly, which pleased the blind man, and he said, "I can give you neither gold nor silver, but I can teach you much in the ways of getting a livelihood." It was so that, after a few days, he showed me many things, and being blind himself, he enlightened and guided me in the ways of life. Wonderful sagacity and cleverness of the blind man. I mention these trifles to your Honour to show how much knowledge men must have when they are down, and to keep from falling when they are exalted.

Speaking of the good there was in my blind man, your Honour must know that since God created the world He has not made a being more astute and sagacious. In his own line he was unequalled. He knew a hundred or more prayers of the choir, he recited in a low and very tuneful voice, he put on a devout and very humble countenance when he recited, without making faces or gestures as others usually do. Besides this he had a hundred other ways and means of getting money. He knew how to make prayers on different occasions, for women who were childless, for those who were about to bear children, and for those who had married unhappily, that their husbands might like them well. He foretold whether a woman would have a boy or a girl. In the matter of medicine he said that Galen did not possess half his knowledge for curing toothaches, fainting fits, or illnesses of mothers. Finally, no one mentioned what pain or illness he or she was suffering from, but he told them at once—do this, you should do that, gather such a herb, take such a root. In this way he went with all the world after him, especially the women. They believed whatever he said, and from them he drew great profits by the arts I have described, for he gained more in a month than a hundred other blind men would in a year. I also desire that your Honour should know that, in spite of all he acquired and had, I never met a man so avaricious and stingy, insomuch that he nearly killed me with hunger, depriving me of the necessaries of life.

I tell the truth, that if, by way of subtlety and cunning, I had not found a remedy, I *The blind* should many times have succumbed *man's way of* to starvation. With all his know- *making money* *and his avarice.* ledge and experience, I managed so well that, oftener than not, I got the best of it. On account of these matters, there were infernal rows between us, of which I will relate some but not all.

He carried the bread, and all the rest of his things, in a linen knapsack, closing the mouth with an iron chain having a padlock and key. He put in and took out his things himself, using great vigilance, and he kept such a close account that there was not a man in all the world who could have taken *Lazaro finds his way into* so much as a crumb without his *the blind man's* knowing it. Well, I had to take the *knapsack.* lazar's allowance which he gave me. It was all despatched in less than two mouthfuls. After he had locked the bag and was not looking out, thinking that I was attending to other things, by a little unstitching I often opened one side of the bag and sewed it up again ; bleeding the avaricious knapsack not only of bread but of good pieces of bacon and sausage. Thus I watched for convenient times to make up for the infernal wrong that the wicked blind man inflicted on me.

All that I could pilfer and steal I carried in half " blancas." When they paid him for saying prayers for them, they gave *Lazaro's adroit* him a whole " blanca." But as he *contrivance with the half* could not see, I had got it in my *" blancas."* mouth, and put a half blanca in its place, before his hand had reached it, quick as he was, so that he only got half-price. The evil-minded blind man complained when he found that it was not a whole "blanca." He said to me : " How the devil is it that since you have been with me they only give half 'blancas,' and before it used to be a whole 'blanca' or even a 'maravedi' that they gave me ?[1] The ill-luck has come with you." So he shortened up the prayers and did not give them more than half, ordering me to remind him to stop by pulling his sleeve. Then he began to cry out that they had called for such and such a prayer from him, such as he used to recite, and that he had given it.

The blind man used to have a small jug of wine near him when he dined ; and quick as *Various ways of getting at the wine.* thought I gave it silent kisses when I put it down for him. But it was not long before he noticed the loss in what he drank, so he never let the jug out of his hand, but always kept it by him. How-

[1] The copper *maravedi* was a coin the value of which varied. It may be taken as a penny. The *blanca* was so called from the whiteness of the metal of which it was made. In the time of Alonso XI. there were three blancas to the maravedi. From 1497 the maravedi was worth two blancas. The great dictionary of the Spanish Academy quotes *Lazarillo de Tormes* as the authority for the value of the blanca and half blanca, or farthing.

ever, he had no magnet to point to what went on, while I had a long oaten straw which I prepared for this need of mine. Slipping it into the mouth of the jug I sucked up the wine to my heart's content. The old rascal, being very astute, suspected something. So he put the jug between his knees and, covering the mouth with his hand, drank in security. Seeing the wine go I craved for it. The straw being no longer of any avail, I hit upon another plan. I succeeded in making a tiny hole in the bottom of the jug, and stopped it with a small piece of wax. When dinner-time came I pretended to be cold, and got between the old man's legs, to warm myself at the poor little light we had. With the same light I melted the wax, and very soon a little fountain began to drain into my mouth, which I placed so that I should not lose a drop. When the poor old man wanted to drink he got nothing. His astonishment was expressed in curses, devoting the wine and the jug to the devil. "You cannot think that I have been drinking, uncle!" I said, "for you have not let the jug out of your hand." But he gave the jug so many twists and turns that at last he found the hole. He said nothing. Next day I was sucking at my hole as usual, thinking no evil,

The wicked blind man's cruel revenge.

and little dreaming of what he was getting ready for me. I was seated on the ground, taking in those delicious draughts, my face turned up to heaven, my eyes half closed the better to enjoy the toothsome liquor, when the wicked blind man took his revenge. He raised the jug with both hands, and, with all his might, sent it crashing down on my mouth. Poor Lazaro was quite off his guard, being careless and joyous as at other times. Truly it seemed to me as if the sky and all that was in it had fallen upon me. The blow was so great that the pieces of the jug cut my face in several parts and broke my teeth, so that I remain without them to this day.

From that time I wished evil to the cruel blind man, and, although he was kind to me afterwards and cured me, I saw very well that he enjoyed my cruel punishment. He washed the bruises and places torn by the bits of the broken jug, but he smiled as he did so, saying, " What would you have, Lazaro ? If I wish you ill I cure you and restore you to health," with other jokes which were not to my taste, when I had only half recovered from my wounds. I now wanted to free myself from him, thinking that a few more such blows might free him from me. He was not much inclined to see to my

A coolness arises between Lazaro and the blind man.

health and welfare, and even if I had wished to forgive him the blow with the jug, his evil treatment of me from that time would have prevented it.

Without cause or reason, the malignant blind man was always beating me and knocking me about. If any one asked him why he treated me so badly, he told the story of the jug, adding : "Think you that my boy is a little innocent? Well, listen and judge whether the devil himself could have played such tricks. Who could believe that such a small boy could be so depraved." Then they said : "Chastise him in God's name," and he never did anything else.

So I led him by the worst ways, seeking to do him harm, taking him over stony places and into mud. He always beat me *Lazaro is beaten, so the blind man is led into the mud.* on the back of my head, so that it was covered with bruises, and although I cried out that I did not do it on purpose, but only because there was no better road, he did not believe me, such was the astuteness and intelligence of the old ruffian.

In order that your Honour may judge of the cleverness of this knowing old man I will relate one thing out of many that happened while I was with him. When we left

Salamanca his intention was to go to Toledo, for he said that the people there were richer, though not very charitable. He repeated this saying, "The hard man gives more than the penniless man." We took the road by the best places, where we were well received. It happened that we came to a place called Almorox[1] at the time of the vintage. A grape-gatherer gave us a bunch out of charity. As the baskets are knocked about, and the grapes at that time are very hard, the blind man kept the bunch in his hand and, to content me, he determined to have a banquet with it, instead of putting it in his bag. For on that day he had given me many blows and kicks.

We sat down in an enclosed place and he said : "Now I am going to treat you with *The way* liberality. We will both eat this *Lazaro and the* bunch of grapes in equal shares, and *blind man* *shared a bunch* it shall be in this way. You take *of grapes.* one and I will take another. You must only take one at a time, and I will take another until it is finished. In this way there can be no trick." So we began. At the

---

[1] Almorox is a village with three hundred houses formed in irregular streets and an open square. The church of San Cristoval has a fine north door. The place belonged to the Duke of Escalona. Its vineyards produce wine like Valdepeñas. It is about twelve miles from the town of Escalona.

second turn the old traitor began to take two at a time. As he had broken the agreement I thought that I ought to do the same. Not content to do as he did, I began to take three at a time. When the bunch was finished, he sat for some time with the stalk in his hand. Then he said, "Lazaro, you have deceived me. I would swear to God that you have been eating three at a time." "I did not eat so," I declared. "Why do you suspect me?" "Would you know how I am certain that you took three at a time?" he replied. "It is because when I began to take two at a time you said nothing."

Though only a boy I noted the cleverness of the old man. But to avoid being dull I will leave out many things both curious and remarkable that happened to me while I was with my first master, for I wish to come to the leave-taking, and with that there is an end of him.

An example of the blind man's cleverness.

We were at Escalona,[1] a town belonging

[1] The Duke of Escalona was the maternal grandfather of the author. The town of Escalona is on the right bank of the river Alberche, and about one hundred feet above it. Escalona is twenty-five miles north-west of Toledo. It was surrounded by a wall ten feet thick and thirty feet high, with two gates. In the principal square there were arcades and a stone cross. Juan II. gave Escalona to the Constable Alvaro de Luna in 1424, who built a great palace there, which was demolished by the French under Marshal Soult. King Henry IV. gave Escalona to Juan Pacheco,

to the Duke of that name, lodging at an inn.

The blind man gave me a piece of sausage to roast. When the sausage had been basted Lazaro falls and the toasted bread on which the into temptation and eats the grease was poured had been eaten, sausage. he took a maravedi out of his bag and sent me to fetch wine from a tavern. The devil put the temptation before my eyes, which, as they say, is how a thief is made. There was also a long piece of colewort[1] on the fire, which, being unfit for the pot, ought to have been thrown away. There was nobody but the blind man and myself, and I became very greedy under the delicious smell of the sausage. I only thought of present enjoyment, without considering what might happen afterwards. As the blind man took the money out of his bag, I took the sausage,

the Master of Santiago. In Lazarillo's time it belonged to Don Diego Lopez de Pacheco, second Duke of Escalona and Marquis of Villena. He distinguished himself in the last Moorish war in Granada, and died in 1529. He resided in the old palace built by the Constable Alvaro de Luna, where he dispensed hospitality, among many others to Don Alonzo Enriquez de Guzman (see translation of that young adventurer's life and acts, p. 71, Hakluyt Society, 1862). Madoz states that, in his time, Escalona consisted of 190 houses, population 580.

[1] *Navo*, called colewort in the Neuman and Baretti dictionary. More likely what Gervase Markham (*Country Farm*, p. 185) calls "navet," a sort of small turnip.

and quickly put the colewort to be cooked in its place. When my master handed the money to me I took it, and went for the wine, not failing to eat the sausage.

When the sinful blind man found the colewort in the pot, of which he knew nothing, he thought it was the sausage and bit it. Then he said, "What is this, Lazaro?" I said "Had I not gone for the wine? Some one else has been here and has done it for fun." "No! No!" he cried, "that is impossible, for I have never let the pan out of my hand." I then turned to swear, and swore again, that it was not me. But it availed me nothing. From the cunning of the cursed blind man nothing could be hidden.

My master got up and took me by the head. Presently he began to smell me, and forcing my mouth open, he put his nose in. It was a long pointed nose. What with the turn I had, the choke Dreadful trouble about the sausage. in my throat, and the fright I was in, the sausage would not stay on my stomach, and the whole thing came back to its owner. The evil blind man so worked my inside that the half-masticated sausage and the long nose came out of my mouth together. O Lord! who would not rather have been buried than go through that misery? The rage of the perverse old man was such that if people had not been drawn there by the noise, he would not have left me alive. They took me from him, leaving his few hairs in my hands, and his face and throat all scratched, which he deserved for his cruel treatment of me.

The blind man related all my misfortunes over and over again, including the story of the jug and of the bunch of grapes. The laughter was so loud that all the passers-by came in to see the fun ; for the old wretch told the stories of my misfortunes so well that even I, ill-treated as I was, could not help half joining in the laughter. Remembering my troubles there came a weakness upon me. But my stomach recovered, and the landlady of the inn, with others who were present, washed my face and throat with the wine that had been brought to drink. This enraged the wicked blind man, who declared that I would cost him more wine with my washings in one year, than he could drink in two.

Lazaro recovers from the effects of the sausage.

"Lazaro," he said, "you owe more to the wine than to your father. He got you once, but the wine has brought you to life several times." Then he counted how many times he had torn and bruised my face and afterwards cured it with wine.

26

"If there is a man in the world who ought to be lucky with wine," he added, "it is you."

Those who were washing me laughed a good deal at what the old man said, though I dissented. However, the prognostications of the blind rascal did not turn out false, and afterwards I often thought of that man, who certainly had the spirit of prophecy.[1] The evil things he did to me made me sad, though I paid him back, as your Honour will presently hear.

Seeing all this, and how the blind man made me a laughing-stock, I determined that at all hazards I would leave him. Lazaro determined to leave This resolution was always in my the blind man. mind, and the last game he played confirmed it. On another day we left the town to seek alms. It had rained a great deal in the previous night. It continued to rain in the day-time, and we got under some arcades in that town, so as to keep out of the wet. Night was coming on and the rain did not cease. The blind man said to me, "Lazaro! this rain is very persistent, and as the night closes in it will not cease, so we will make for the inn in good time. To go there we have to cross a stream which will have become swollen by the heavy rain." I replied,

[1] See p. 98.

"Uncle ! the stream is now very broad, but if you like I can take you to a place where we

Lazaro prepares to revenge himself on the blind man.

can get across without being wet, for it becomes much narrower, and by jumping we can clear it." This seemed good advice, so he said, "You are discreet and you shall take me to that place where the stream becomes so narrow, for it is winter time, and a bad thing to get our feet wet." Seeing that things were going as I wished, I took him out of the arcade, and placed him just in front of a stone pillar that stood in the square. Then I said to him, "Uncle, this is the narrowest part of the stream."

As the rain continued and he was getting wet, we were in a hurry to get shelter from

Lazaro's cruel vengeance on the blind man.

the water that was falling upon us. The principal thing was (seeing that God blinded my understanding in that hour) to be avenged. The old man believed in me and said, "Put me in the right place while you jump over the stream." So I put him just in front of the pillar, and placed myself behind it. I then said, "Jump with all your might so as to clear the stream." I had hardly finished speaking, when the poor old man, balancing himself like a goat, gave one step backwards, and then sprang with all

his force.   His head came with such a noise
against the pillar that it sounded like a great
calabash.   He fell down half dead.   " How
was it you could smell the sausage Lazaro leaves
and not the post ?   Oh ! Oh ! "   I his first master.
shouted.   I left him among several people
who ran to help him, while I made for the gate
of the town at a sharp trot, so that before
nightfall I might be in Torrijos, not knowing nor caring what afterwards happened to
my blind man.[1]

[1] The "pillar" was a stone cross which still stands in the
plaza of Escalona.

SECOND MASTER

HOW LAZARO TOOK SERVICE WITH A CLERGY-MAN, AND OF THE THINGS THAT HAPPENED TO HIM.

NEXT day, as I did not feel that I should be quite safe at Torrijos,[1] I stopped at a place called Maqueda,[2] where for my sins I took service with a clergyman. Going to him to ask for alms, he inquired

The clergyman's chest.

---

[1] Torrijos is sixteen miles north-west of Toledo, and eight miles from the Tagus, in a valley on the road from Maqueda to Toledo. It was walled, and still has two old gateways. Madoz gives it 480 houses, and in the plaza is the palace of the Count of Altamira, built of stone. The church is dedicated to San Gil. Here Beatriz, the daughter of King Pedro by Maria de Padilla, was born in 1353. The country round yields abundant oil, and the place is sometimes called Torrijos de los Olivares.

[2] Maqueda is six leagues north-west of Toledo, built on a hill, on the margin of a stream of the same name which falls into the Alberche, a tributary of the Tagus. It has 112 houses, scattered along badly paved dirty streets. There is an old castle, and two churches, San Juan Bantista and San Domingo. Water is abundant. Maqueda was taken from the Moors by Alfonso VI. in 1083, and in 1177 it was granted to the knights of Calatrava. Ferdinand and Isabella made Diego de Cardenas Duke of Maqueda.

whether I knew how to assist at Mass. I said
yes, which was true, for though the blind man
ill-treated me, he taught me many useful
things, and one of them was this. Finally the
clergyman took me as his servant. Out of the
I had escaped from the thunder frying-pan
to fall under the lightning. For into the fire.
compared with this priest, the blind man was
an Alexander the Great. I will say no more
than that all the avarice in the world was
combined in this man, but I know not whether
it was naturally born in him or whether it
was put on with the priestly habit. He had
an old chest closed with a key which he
carried with him, fastened to the belt of his
gown. When he brought the " bodigos "[1]
from the church, they were quickly locked up
in the chest, and there was nothing to eat in
the house such as is to be seen in other houses,
a piece of bacon, some bits of cheese on a shelf
or in a cupboard, or a few pieces of bread that
may have remained over from the table. It
seemed to me that the sight of such things,
even if I could not have them, would have
been a consolation.

There was only a string of onions, and these

[1] Small loaves made of the finest flour, offered to the Church.
The Dictionary of the Spanish Academy quotes Lazarillo de
Tormes as the authority for the meaning of this word.

were under lock and key in an upper chamber,

one being allowed for every four days. If I asked for the key, to fetch the allowance, and any one else was present, he put his hand in his pocket, and gave it to me with great ceremony, telling me to take it and return at once without taking anything else ; as if all the conserves of Valencia were there. Yet there was not a thing in the room but the onions hanging from a nail, and he kept such a strict account of them, that if I ever took more than my allowance it cost me dear. At last I was near dead with hunger.

If he showed little charity to me, he treated himself as badly. Small bits of meat formed his usual food for dinner and supper. It is true that he shared the gravy with me, but nothing more except a small piece of bread. On Saturdays they eat sheep's head in those parts, and my master sent me for one that was to cost three maravedis. He cooked it and ate all the eyes, tongue, brains, and the meat off the cheeks, giving me the well-picked bone on a plate, and saying, "Take ! Eat ! Triumph ! for you is the world, and you live better than the Pope." At the end of three weeks I became so weak that I could scarcely stand on my feet for hunger. I saw myself sinking down into the silent tomb. If God and my own intelligence had not enabled me to avail myself of in- genious tricks, there would have been no remedy for me.

Lazaro was sinking into the silent tomb from hunger.

When we were at the offertory not a single blanca was dropped into the shell without being registered by him. He kept one eye on the congregation and the other on my hands, moving his eyes about as if they were quicksilver. He knew exactly how many blancas had been given, and as soon as the offertory was over, he took the shell from me and put it on the altar. During all the time I lived, or rather was dying in his service, I never was master of a single blanca. I never brought a blanca worth of wine from a tavern, but it was put into his chest to last for a week. To conceal his extreme stinginess he said to me, " Look here, boy ! Priests have to be very frugal in eating and drinking, and for this reason I do not feed like other people." But he lied shamefully. For at meetings and funerals where we had to say prayers and responses, and where he could get food at the expense of others, he ate like a wolf and drank more than a proposer of toasts.

Extraordinary stinginess of the clergyman.

And why do I speak of funerals ? God

forgive me ! for I never was an enemy to the human race except on those occasions. Then we could eat well, and I wished, and even prayed to God that He would kill some one every day.

When we gave the Sacraments to the sick, especially extreme unction, the priest was called upon to say prayers for those who were present. I was certainly not the last in prayer, for with all my heart I besought the Lord that He would take the sick man to Himself. If any one recovered I devoted him to the devil a thousand times. He who died received many benedictions from me, yet the number of persons who died during the whole time I was there, which was over six months, only amounted to twenty. I verily believed that I killed them, or rather that they died in answer to my prayers, the Lord seeing how near death I was, and that their deaths gave me life.

But there was no remedy, for if on the days of the funerals I lived, on the days when no one died I was starving, and I felt it all the more. So that there seemed to be no rest for me but in death ; and I often desired it for myself, as well as for others.

I frequently thought of leaving my penurious master, but two things detained me. The first was that I feared my legs would not carry me, so reduced was I by starvation. The other was the consideration that I had had two masters. The first starved me, the second brought me to death's door, and a third might finish me. It appeared that any change might be for the worse.

One day when my wretched master was out, a locksmith came to the door by chance. I thought that he was an angel sent Lazaro is saved to me by the hand of God, in the from starvation by an angel of dress of a workman. He asked me a locksmith. whether I had any work for him to do. Inspired by the Holy Spirit I replied : " Uncle ! I have lost a key, and I fear that my master will whip me. Kindly see if there are any on your bunch that will fit the lock, and I will pay you for it." The angelic locksmith began to try his keys, and soon the chest was opened, and I beheld the Lord's gift The chest in the form of bread. " I have no opened. money," I said, " to give you for the key, but take what you like in payment." He took one of the loaves that looked the best, and went away quite satisfied, leaving the key with me. I did not touch anything, at the moment, because I did not feel the need. My wretched master came back, and, as God willed

35

it, he did not look into the trunk which that
angel had opened. But next day, when he
had gone out, I opened my bread paradise
Lazaro is happy and took a loaf between the hands
until the clergy-
man begins to and teeth. In two *credos* I made it
smell a rat. invisible. Not forgetting the open
chest, I rejoiced to think that, with this
remedy, my life would be less miserable.
Thus I was happy with him for two days, but
it was not destined that this should continue.
For on the third day, at the very time that
The clergyman I was dying of hunger, he was to be
counts the seen at our chest, counting and re-
loaves of bread. counting the loaves. I dissimulated,
and, in my secret prayers and devotions, I
implored that he might be blinded. After he
had been counting for a long time, he said :
"If I did not keep such an exact account I
should think that some loaves have been taken
from this chest. From this day I shall have
a more accurate account. There are now
nine loaves and part of another." "New misfortunes have come," I said to myself, and I
felt that my stomach would soon be in the
same wretched state as before.

When the priest went out, I opened the
chest as some consolation, and when I saw the
bread I began to worship it, giving it a
thousand kisses. But I did not pass that day

so happily as the day before. As my hunger increased, so did my longing for more bread. At length God, who helps the afflicted, showed me a remedy. I said to myself : " This chest is old, and broken in some parts, though the holes are very small. The belief might be suggested that rats had got through these holes and had eaten some of the bread." It would not do to eat wholesale, but I began to crumble the bread over some not very valuable cloth, taking some and leaving some, and thus I got a meal. When the priest came to examine the damage, he did not doubt that it had been done by the rats, because it seemed to be done just in the way that rats would do it. He looked over the chest from one end to the other, and saw the holes by which the rats might have entered.

He then called to me and said : " Lazaro, look ! Look what damage has been done to our bread last night ! " I appeared to be much astonished, and wondered how it could have happened. " It is the rats," he declared, "they would leave us nothing." We went to our meal, and even there it pleased God that I should come off well ; for he gave me more than usual, including all the parts he thought the rats had touched, saying : " Eat

It was the rats.

37

this which the rat has cleaned." Thus the
work of my hands, or rather nails, was added
to my allowance.

Presently I beheld another piece of work.
The wretched priest was pulling nails out of
The clergyman boards up all the rat holes in the old chest. the wall, and looking for small
boards with which to cover all the
holes in the ancient chest. "O
Lord!" I then said to myself, "to what
miseries and disasters are we born, and how
brief are our pleasures in this our toilsome
life! I thought that by this poor little contrivance I might find a way to pass out of
my misery, and I even ventured to rejoice at
my good-fortune, and now my ill-luck has
returned." Using all the diligence in his
power, for misers as a rule are not wanting
in that commodity, he shut the door of my
consolation while he boarded up the holes in
the chest. Thus I made my lamentation, as
an end was made to the work, with many
small boards and nails. "Now," said the
priest, "the traitor rats will find little in this
house, and had better leave us, for there is
not a hole left large enough for a mosquito
to get in."

When he was gone I opened the chest with
my key without any hope of profit from doing
so. There were the three or four loaves

"' It is the rats,' he declared."

which my master thought the rats had not begun upon. Night and day I thought of some other plan, with the help of my hunger, for they say that it is an aid to invention. It certainly was so with me. One night I was deep in thought, meditating how I might use the contents of the chest again. My master was snoring loudly, so I took an old knife and went to the chest. I used the knife in the way of a gimlet, and as the ancient piece of furniture was without strength or heart, it soon surrendered, and allowed me to make a nice hole. This done I opened the chest, had a good meal, and went back to my straw bed, where I rested and slept.

Next day my master saw both the hole and the damage done to his provisions. He began to commend the rats to the devil, saying, " What shall we say to this ! Never have I known rats in this house until now." He may well have spoken the truth, for such creatures do not stay where there is nothing to eat. He turned to find more nails in the wall, and a small board to cover the hole. Night came and he retired to rest, while I set to work to open by night what he had closed up in the day. It was like the weaving of Penelope, for all he did by day I undid by night. In a few days we got

What the clergyman did by day, Lazaro undid by night.

41

the poor old chest into such a state, that it might be described as a sieve of old time rather than a chest.

When the miserly priest saw that his remedies were of no use he said : " This chest is so knocked about, and the wood is so old and weak that there is not a rat against which it can be defended. We will leave it without defence outside, and I will go to the cost of three or four reals. As the best outside guard is no use, I will attack these cursed rats from the inside." He presently borrowed a rat-trap, and begged some pieces of cheese from the neighbours. This was a great help to me. In truth I did not need much sauce for my bread, still, I enjoyed the bits of cheese which I got from the rat-trap.

When he found the bread eaten in rat's fashion, the cheese gone, and no rats caught, The rat-trap adds cheese to Lazaro's bread. he again commended the rats to the devil. He asked the neighbours how the cheese could have been taken without the rat being caught. They agreed that it could not have been a rat. One neighbour remembered that there used to be a snake in the house, and they all concurred that it must have been the snake. As it is long it could have taken the cheese without being caught in the trap. This exercised the

42

mind of my master very much, and from that time he slept so lightly that the slightest sound made him think that the snake was going into the chest. Then he would jump up and give the chest many violent blows with a stick, intending to frighten the snake. The noise used to awaken the neighbours, while I could not sleep. He rolled about my straw, and me with it, because the neighbours said that snakes liked to keep warm It must have in the straw, or in cradles where been a snake. there are babies, where they even bit them and were dangerous. I generally went to sleep again, and he told me about it in the morning, saying : " Did you feel nothing last night, my boy ? I was after the snake, and I even think it came to your bed, for when snakes are cold they seek for warmth." I replied, " It was lucky it did not bite me, but I am terribly frightened." I did not get up or go to the chest at night, but waited until my master was in church. He used to see the inroads on his bread, but knew not how to apply a remedy.

I began to be afraid that, with all my diligence, he might find my key which I kept amongst the straw. I thought it would be safer to put it in my mouth. For when I lived with the blind man I used my mouth

as a purse, keeping ten or twelve maravedis
Lazaro determined to keep the key in his mouth—a fatal mistake. in it, all in half blancas, without being prevented from eating. Without that plan I could not have kept a blanca from the knowledge of the cursed blind man, for I had not a seam or a lining which he did not examine very minutely. So, as I have said, I put the key in my mouth every night, and slept without fear that my wizard of a master would find it. But when misfortune comes, wit and diligence are of no avail.

It chanced, owing to ill-luck, or rather owing to my sins, that I was sleeping one night with the key in my mouth in such a position that the air went out of the hollow in the key and caused it to whistle so that, for my sins, my master heard it. So he got up with the club in his hand, and came to me very quietly that the snake might not hear, for he felt no doubt that it was the snake. He thought that it was in the straw, and he raised the club with the intention of giving it such a blow as to kill it. So he hit me on the head with all his force and left me senseless.

Seeing the quantity of blood he understood the harm he had done me, and went in a great hurry to get a light. Coming back he found me with the key in my mouth, half of it projecting, in the same way as it was when I was whistling with it. The killer of Lazaro is found out, and half killed in the process. snakes was astounded that it should have been the key. He took it out of my mouth to see what it was. Then he went to try it in the lock, and found out my practices. He said that the rats and the snake that devoured his substance were found. What happened in the next three days I know not, for I was in the belly of the whale. At the end of that time my senses returned. I found myself lying on my straw, and my head covered with unguents and plasters. I was astounded and said: "What is this?" The cruel priest answered that he had caught the rats and the serpent. Finding myself so evilly treated, I began to understand what had happened. At this time an old woman came in and dressed my wound. Then the neighbours began to take off the Lazaro recovers and is shown the door. bandages. They rejoiced when they saw that I had recovered my senses, and began to laugh over my misfortunes while I, as the sinner, mourned over them. With all this they gave me something to eat, so that in a fortnight I could get up and was out of danger, though suffering from hunger. On another day, when I was up, my master took me by the hand and put me outside the door.

Being in the street, he said : " From to-day,
Lazaro, you are your own master and not my
servant. Seek another master, and go, in God's
name ; for I do not want such a diligent
person in my service, who is only fit to be a
blind man's guide." He then crossed himself
as if he thought I had a devil, went back into
the house, and shut the door.

THIRD MASTER

HOW LAZARO TOOK SERVICE WITH A GENTLE-MAN, AND WHAT HAPPENED TO HIM

THUS I was obliged to seek strength out of weakness, and little by little, with the help of kind people, I reached this famous *Lazaro reaches* city of Toledo. At the end of fifteen *Toledo, and seeks for a* days, by the mercy of God, my wound *master.* was healed. While I was ill people gave me some alms, but as soon as I was well they all said, " You lazy little vagabond, go and seek for a master whom you may serve." " But where can I find one ? " I said to myself.

I was wandering about from door to door, without any settled purpose, when I came upon an esquire,[1] who was walking *On the road* down the street, fairly well dressed *to Toledo.* and groomed. He looked at me and I at

[1] Escudero. The English equivalent is *esquire*; Latin, *armiger*. Selden says that the original of this title was the office or function of *armiger* or *scutifer*. Our *esquire* and the French *escuyer* are derived from Scutarius. In Froissart we have knights and esquires, in Spain cavalleros (knights) and escuderos (esquires).

him. He then said, "Boy! are you seeking for a master?" I replied, "Yes, sir!" The esquire. "Then come along behind me," he said, "for God has shown mercy to you by letting you meet with me." So I followed him, giving thanks to God. Judging from his dress and manner I thought he was the sort of master of whom I stood in need.

It was in the morning when I met with my third master, and I followed him over Lazaro enters the service of an esquire. a great part of the city. He passed by the place where they sell bread and other provisions, and I thought and desired that he would employ me to carry what he bought, for it was the time for marketing. But, with a slow step, he passed by all these things. Perhaps, I thought, he is not satisfied with them and intends to make his purchases in some other place. In this way we walked about until eleven in the forenoon, when he entered the principal church, and I at his heels. I saw him hear Mass and the other divine offices very devoutly until the service was all finished, and the people had gone. Then we left the church and began to walk down the street. I was the happiest boy in the world to see that my master had not troubled himself about

"*I followed him over a great part of the city.*"

marketing, for I deduced from that the belief
that he had everything at home, where I
should find all that I desired. At last we
came to a house before which my master
stopped, and I with him.

Throwing the end of his cloak over his left
shoulder, he took a key out of his sleeve and
opened the door. We entered the *The esquire*
house. It was so dark and dismal *takes Lazaro*
that it might cause fear to any one *to his house.*
coming in. Within there was a small court
and fair-sized rooms. He then took off his
cloak and, first asking whether I had clean
hands, he shook it and folded it. Then, after
very carefully blowing the dust off a bench
that was there, he put the cloak on it.
Having done this he sat upon it and began to
ask me questions, in great detail, as to where
I came from and how I reached the city. I
had to give him a much longer account than
I cared for, as it seemed to me that it was
a more convenient time for laying the cloth
and getting the meal ready than for answering
what he asked. Nevertheless, I satisfied his
curiosity with the best lies I could *Nothing to eat*
invent, relating all I had done well, *in the esquire's*
and holding my tongue about the *house.*
rest, which did not appear to me to be appro-
priate. This done, we remained in the same

51

place for a while. It was now nearly two o'clock in the afternoon, and there was no more sign of anything to eat than there would be for the dead.

After this my master closed the door and locked it, and neither above nor below was there a sign of any other person in the house. All I had seen was walls, without chairs or table, or even a chest, like that of the rats and snake. It was like a house bewitched. At this juncture he said to me, " You, my boy ! have you eaten? " " No, sir," said I, "for it was not eight o'clock when I met your worship." " Well," he said, " although I have breakfasted this morning, I shall be fasting until night, so you must hold on, and afterwards we will have supper." When I heard this I was very much depressed, not so much from hunger, as from the knowledge that the luck was continuing to be against me. For my hardships seemed to be coming back. I mourned over my troubles, and remembered what I once thought, when I was meditating on leaving the priest, that ill-fortune might bring me to something worse. Finally, I began to weep over my miserable past life, and over my approaching death. At the same time I dissimulated as well as I could.

Lazaro sees trouble ahead about food, but he dissimulates.

"Sir," I said, "I am a boy who does not trouble much about eating, blessed be God! So that I am able to receive praise among all my equals, as the one who has the most moderate appetite, and for this I have even been praised, up to this time, by my former masters." "This is a virtue," he replied, "and for this I like you better. Gluttony is for pigs and to eat with moderation for respectable people." "Well do I understand you," said I to myself, "and cursed be such medicine, and such kindness as I have had from my masters, who give me nothing but starvation."

I then put myself in one corner of the doorway, and took some pieces of bread out of my bosom, which remained from what had been given me. When he saw it he said to me, "Come here, my boy, what is it you are eating?" I came to him and showed him. *The esquire and Lazaro sup on the boy's three pieces of bread.* He took for himself the largest of the three pieces I had, and said to me, "By my life! this bread seems good." "And sir," said I, "it is good." "Yes, by my faith!" said he, "where did you get it from—are you sure it was kneaded with clean hands?" "I do not know that," said I, "but the smell of it does not turn my stomach." "Please God!" said

53

my poor master, and, putting it to his mouth,
he began to take as voracious mouthfuls as I
did with mine. "It is most delicious," he
said. I feared he would finish first, and that
he would want to help me with what was left
of mine, so we both came to an end at the
same time. My master then began to collect
with his hand a few crumbs which had
remained on our breasts. Then he went into
A meagre a small room and brought out a jug
supper and a without a spout, and not very new.
wretched bed. After he had had a drink he offered
it to me. I said, "Sir! I do not drink
wine." "It is water," he replied, "and you
can well drink it." Then I took the jug and
drank, but not very much, as thirst was not
my complaint. So we remained until the
night, talking about things he had asked me,
while I gave the best answers I could.

He took me into the chamber out of which
he had brought the jug of water, and said,
"Boy, stay here, and see how we make this
bed, that you may know how to make it
henceforward." He put me at one end and
himself at the other, and he made the miserable bed. There was not much to make.
He had a sort of hurdle on trestles. Over
this he spread clothes. They did not look
very like a mattress, but served as one, with

much less blanket than was necessary. What there was we spread out, but it was impossible to soften the bed. It was too hard.

When the bed was made, and the night being come, he said to me : "Lazaro, it is now too late, it is a long way to the market-place, and in this city there are many thieves who prowl about at night. We must do the best we can, and to-morrow, when it is light, God will have mercy. Being alone I am not provided, for I have been in the habit of having my meals outside, but now we will arrange things in another way." "Sir," I replied, "do not trouble about me, for I can pass a night like this." "You will become more and more healthy," he then told me, "for there is nothing in the world that lives long but it eats little." "If that is so," I said to myself, "I shall never die, for I have always been obliged to observe that rule by force, and even, if my ill-luck continues, it may be so all my life."

The esquire's apology for no supper. His philosophical view of starvation.

He lay down on the bed, using his hose and doublet for a pillow, and ordered me to put myself at his feet. I did so, but not to go to sleep, for the canes of the hurdle and my protruding bones struggled with each other without ceasing. What with

A very bad night.

my hardships, misery, and starvation I do not think there was a pound's weight of flesh on my body. As I had scarcely eaten anything all day I was wild with hunger, which is not a friend of sleep. I cursed my fate and my ill-luck a thousand times, may God pardon me! I was like that most of the night, not daring to turn for fear of awakening my master; and I prayed to God many times for death.

When morning came we got up and began to shake and brush the doublet and hose, the coat and cloak. My master dressed himself very carefully, combed his hair, washed his hands, and put his sword on. As he did so he said to me : "Ah, my boy, if you only knew what a weapon this sword is. There is not a mark of gold in the whole world for which I would give it. Moreover, there is not a sword among all that Antonio ever made that has the steel so tempered as this one." Then he drew it out and tried it with his finger, saying, "Look here, I am obliged to use a ball of wool for it." I said to myself, "And I need a piece of bread for my teeth, though they are not made of steel." He put his sword back, and with a stately pace, his body erect, his head turned gently from side to side, throwing

The esquire attends to his outward appearance.

"What there was we spread out."

the end of his cloak over his shoulder, and putting his right hand on his side, he said, "Lazaro, take care of the house, make the bed, fetch water from the river for the jug, as it is getting low. I am going to hear Mass. Lock the door that nothing may be stolen, placing the key on the hook by the hinge, that I may be able to come in when I return."

He then marched down the street with such a contained and noble air that any one who did not know the contrary *Stately* would have thought that he was a *appearance of* very near relation to the Count of *the esquire* *when he walked* Arcos,[1] or at least his chamberlain *abroad.* who had been clothed by him. "A blessing on you, my lord," I was left saying, "who gives the disease and provides the remedy." Who would meet my master, and, judging from his satisfied look, not suppose *Lazaro's re-* that he had supped well and slept in *flections on the* *secrets hidden* a comfortable bed, and that in the *under the* morning he had had a good break- *esquire's cloak.* fast? Great secrets, sir, are those which you keep and of which the world is ignorant.

---

[1] The Duke of Arcos was a very grand nobleman. The title belonged to the family of Ponce de Leon, but before this was written the head of the family had become Duke of Cadiz, a title which was afterwards changed to that of Duke of Arcos. The second Duke was flourishing at this time, and died in 1590. Count, in the text, is a mistake. It should be Duke.

Who would not be deceived by that fair presence and decent cloak ? And who would think that the same gentleman passed all that day without eating anything but the bit of bread which his servant Lazaro had carried all day in his bosom, where it was not likely to find much cleanliness ? To-day, washing his hands and face, he had to wipe them with the end of his cloak for want of a towel. Certainly no one would have suspected it. O Lord ! how many such as him must be scattered over the world, who suffer for the jade they call honour that which they would not suffer for a friend.

I was standing at the door, looking out and thinking of these and many other things until *Lazaro's re-* my master disappeared down the *flections. He goes for water* long and narrow street. Then I *and finds his* went back into the house, and in the *master flirting on the river* time that it would take to say a *bank.* *credo* I had run all over it without finding anything. I made the hard bed, took up the jug and went with it to the river. There I saw my master in great request with two fair ladies in a garden. There were other ladies, for many think it fashionable to go and refresh themselves on summer mornings by those pleasant banks. In confidence that they will be well received, several gentlemen of the place also frequent the river-side. As I have said, my master was among them, saying the sweetest things that Ovid ever wrote. They had no shame in asking him to pay for their breakfasts, but he, finding that he was as cold in the purse as he was empty in the stomach, began to have that feeling which robs the face of its colour, and to make not very valid excuses. When they saw his infirmity, they went to those who were not suffering from it. I was breaking my fast with some stalks of vegetables with great diligence, and not seeing any more of my master I went back to the house.

I thought of sweeping some part of it, which was very necessary, but I could find nothing with which to do it ; so I set myself to think what I should do next. I thought I would wait for my master until noon. When he came he might by good luck bring something for us to eat. But there was no such experience for me. It was two o'clock, my master had not come, and I was desperately hungry. So I shut the door, put the key where I was told, and gave all my attention to my own necessities.

Lazaro waits long for his master to bring food, but he never came.

With a low and feeble voice, and my hands in my bosom, the good God before my eyes, and

my tongue repeating His Name, I began to pray
for bread at the largest houses and doors I came
upon. As this method was sucked in with my
mother's milk, or I should say that I learnt it
from that great master of it, the blind man, so
good a disciple was I that, although in this
city little is known of charity, nor
had it been an abundant year, I made
such a good haul that, before the
clock struck four, I had several pounds of
bread inside me, and two loaves up my sleeve
and in my bosom. I returned to the house,
and, in passing a tripe-shop, I begged of one of
the shopwomen, who gave me a piece of a
cow's foot and several pieces of boiled tripe.

When I got back to the house my good
master was already there. The cloak was
folded and put on the bench, and he was pacing
up and down. He came up to me, and I
thought he was going to scold me for being
late. He asked me where I had been, and I
said, "Sir! I was here until it struck two.
But when I saw that you were not coming, I
went over the city, to commend myself to the
kind people, and they have given me what you
see." I showed him the bread and the tripe,
which I carried in the end of my skirt. At
this he seemed well pleased and said, "Well, I
waited for you to eat, and when you did not

*Lazaro's success-
ful begging
expedition.*

"Gave me a piece of a cow's foot and several pieces of boiled tripe."

come I ate what there was, but you have done
well in this, for it is better to beg in the name
of God than to steal. He helps me as He sees
fit. I merely charge you that people What touches
must not be told that you live the esquire's
with me, for it touches my honour; honour.
though I well believe that it will be kept secret,
because very few people know me here."

"Do not be troubled about that, sir," I
replied to him, "for cursed be he who asks the
question, and myself if I tell him anything.
No, we shall soon be free from want. When I
saw that nothing good came into this house I
went out. Surely the ground must be bad, or
there must be unlucky houses which bring ill-
luck to those who live in them." "This one
must be so without doubt," he replied. "I
promise you that after a month I will not stay
in it, even if it is given me as my own."

I sat down at the end of the bench, and, that
he might not take me for a glutton, I said
nothing about the meal. I began The esquire
supper, and to bite my bread and longs for a share
tripe. Looking stealthily I saw that of Lazaro's
supper.
my unhappy master could not take his eyes off
my skirt, which served as a plate. May God
have as much pity for me as I had for him! I
could feel what he felt, and have been feeling
so every day. I thought whether it would be

right for me to invite him to share, for as he had told me that he had dined, he might decline the invitation. Finally, I asked that sinner to help me in my work, and to break his fast as he did the day before. He had a better chance, the food being better and my hunger less. It pleased God to comply with my wish, and I even think with his. For as he passed, in walking up and down, he came to me and said : " I assure you, Lazaro, that you have the best grace in eating that I ever saw in any one, and that no one can see you doing it, without having a longing to eat, even when he had no such long- ing before." " The great longing that you have makes you think my way of eating so beautiful," I said to myself, " and causes your wish to help me."

He longed to join me, and I opened a way by saying, " Sir, the good tools make the good *Lazaro's* craftsman. This bread is delicious, *courtesy, tact,* and this cow's foot is so well cooked *and kindness.* and seasoned that there is no one that would not be drawn to it by the smell alone." " Cow's foot, is it ? " he said. " Yes, sir ! " " I tell you that is the best mouthful in the world, there is not even a pheasant that is so good." "Try it, sir ! " said I, " and see whether it is as good as you think." I put on one side the cow's foot and three or four pieces of bread, and he sat down by my side, and began to eat as if he would like to devour every little bone. "This wonderful food is like a hotch-potch," he said. "You eat with the best kind of sauce," I replied. "Before God," said he, "if I had known I would not have eaten a mouthful all day." "Thus the good years avenge me," I said to myself. He asked me for the jug of water, and I gave it to him just as I had brought it. My master had not over-eaten, and it is a sign of this that there was no want of water. We both drank, and went to bed in the same way as the night before, well contented. To avoid prolixity I may say that the same thing went on for the next eight or ten days.

In the mornings my master went out to take the air in the streets with the same satisfied look, leaving poor Lazaro with the head of a wolf. I often reflected on my misfortune that, escaping from the evil masters I had served, and seeking to better myself, I should have found one who not only did not maintain me, but whom I had to support. With all that I liked him well enough, seeing that he could not do better. My feeling was rather of sorrow than of enmity. Often I

Lazaro generously provides his master with a supper.

fared ill in bringing to the house that with which he might be satisfied.

One morning the sad esquire got out of bed in his shirt and went up to the roof of the house. Lazaro examines I quickly searched the hose and the esquire's doublet at the head of the bed, and clothes, and finds nothing. found a small purse of velvet, but there had not been so much as a blanca in it for many a day. "This man," I said to myself, " is really poor, and cannot give what he has not got. The avaricious blind man and the ill-conditioned clergyman, may God reward them both! nearly killed me with hunger, the one with a kiss on the hand, the other with a deceitful tongue. Those it is right for me to detest, but for this poor man to have a tender feeling." God is my witness that even now when I meet with any one dressed like this, and walking with the same pompous air, it makes me sad to think that he Lazaro has a might be suffering what I saw my kindly feeling for his third poor master suffer. With all his master. poverty I liked serving him ; but not the other two masters. I only felt some discontent, for I should have liked him not to be quite so proud, and to have lowered his pretensions just a little when his necessities were so great. But it seems to me that it is a well - established rule among such people to

march with their caps well cocked, though
they have not a blanca to their names. The
Lord have mercy on those who have to die of
this disease !

I was in this condition, passing the life I
have described, when my ill-luck again began
to pursue me. In that land the year Begging
was one which only yielded a bad prohibited.
harvest, so the municipal authorities resolved
that all mendicants should leave the town ;
with the addition that any who remained after
four days should be punished by whipping.
Then the law took effect, and there were
processions of poor people being whipped
down the four streets.

This so frightened me that I did not dare
to transgress by begging. So you may imagine
the abstinence of our house, and the Lazaro is kept
sadness and silence of its inmates. alive by some
We were two or three days without kind shop-girls.
eating a mouthful or speaking a word. Some
young women, sewers of cotton who made
caps and lived near us, kept me alive, for I
had made friends with them. From the little
they had, they gave me enough to keep body
and soul together. I was not so unhappy for
myself as for my forlorn master, who in eight
days never ate a mouthful, at least in the
house. I do not know where he went or

what he had to eat when he went out. I used to see him come back at noon, walking along the street with dignified carriage, thinner than a greyhound of good breed, and with regard to what touched the nonsense he called Master and boy honour, he brought a straw of which in a miserable we had not enough in the house. and starving condition. Coming to the door he would grind his teeth with nothing between them, complaining all the time of his bad lodging and saying: "It is a bad thing to see, and a most unlucky place to have to live in, and while we have to be here it will always be wretchedly sad. We have got to endure it, but I wish that this month was over, so that we might leave it."

Being in this miserable and starving condition, one day, I know not through what The esquire good-fortune or chance, my poor brings home a master became possessed of a real. real, but be- moans his fate. He came to the house with it, as delighted as if he had got all the riches of Venice, and smiling at me with a very joyous expression, he said: "Take it, Lazaro, for God has at length begun to open His hand. Go to the market for bread, meat, and wine, for we will break the Devil's eye. I would further have you to know that I have taken another house, and that we shall not have to be in this wretched one for more than another month. May it be accursed, and he who placed the first tile to build it! O Lord! how have I lived here! Scarcely a drop of wine have I drunk nor a morsel of bread have I eaten, nor have I ever had any rest here, and it looks so sad and forbidding. Go and return quickly, for to-day we will eat like counts."

I took the jug and the real, and giving speed to my feet, I began to run up the street to the market, very joyful and contented. But of what avail if evil fortune always brought anxiety with my joy. So it was on this occasion.

As I ran up the street I was calculating how I could spend the money to the best advantage and most profitably, giving thanks to God that my master had got something to spend. Suddenly I met a funeral with many priests and mourners. I got up against the

Terror of Lazaro, thinking they were bringing a dead body to his house.

wall to let them pass. Presently they came, one in deep mourning, apparently the wife of the deceased, with other women. She was crying with a loud voice and saying, " O my lord and husband, whither are they taking you, to the sad and empty house, to the dark and wretched place, to the house where there is nothing to eat and drink." When I heard this the

71

heaven and earth seemed to be joined together.
I exclaimed, " O unhappy me ! it is to our
house that they are taking this dead body."
I turned back, slipped through the crowd of
people, and ran down the street as fast as I
could to our house.   When I got there I
began to close the door in great
haste, calling on my master to come
and help, and to defend the entrance.

<small>Lazaro bars the door to keep out the dead body.</small>

He was rather surprised, thinking it was something else, and said to me, " What is this, my
boy, what are you making a noise about, what
are you doing, why are you shutting the door
in such a fury ? "   " Oh sir," I cried, " they
are bringing a dead body here ! "   " How do
you know ? " he said.   " I met it in the street,"
I replied, "and the dead man's wife was crying
and shouting, ' My lord and husband, whither
do they take you, to the dark and dismal
house, to the sad and wretched place, to the
house where they never eat nor drink.'   It
must be here, sir, that they are bringing it."
Certainly when my master heard this, though
he had no great reason to be merry, he laughed
so heartily that it was a long time before he
could speak.   By this time I had got the
beam across the door and put my shoulder
against it, to make it more secure.

The people passed with their corpse, and

all the time I pushed against the door, to
prevent them from getting into the house.
At last, when he had had much Lazaro barring the door.
more of laughing than of eating, my
good master said to me, "In truth, Lazaro,
seeing what the widow was saying, you were
right to think as you did. But God has been
good to us, and they have passed. So open,
open, and go and get the food." "Let me
wait, sir, until they are out of the At last the esquire unbars the door, and Lazaro does his marketing.
street," I begged. At last my master
came and opened the door in spite
of me, which was necessary, because
I was so upset with fear and excitement. I
then went out. We ate well on that day, but
I took no pleasure in it, nor did my colour
come back for three more days, while my
master smiled a good deal, whenever he noticed
the state I had been in.

In this way I continued with my third and
poorest master, the esquire, for several succeed-
ing days, always longing to know the reason
of his coming and remaining in this place.
For, from the first day that I took service
with him, I saw that he was a stranger,
from the little intercourse he had with the
inhabitants. At last I accomplished my desire,
and came to know what I wanted. It was
one day when we had eaten reasonably well,

and were rather well satisfied. He told me
about his affairs, and said that he came from
Old Castille. He said he had left
his home for no other reason than
that he had not taken off his cap
to a knight who was his neighbour. "Sir," I
said, "if that was what happened, and he was
greater than you, were you not wrong in not
having doffed your cap first? but he ought
to have taken his off as well." He went on
to say that the knight did take off his cap to
him ; but that he had taken his off first so
many times, that it was well to see what the
other would do. "It seems to me, sir," said
I, "that you should have doffed to one greater
and richer than yourself." "You are only a
boy," he replied, "and cannot understand the things appertaining to
honour in which, at the present
time, is all the wealth of respectable people.
You must remember that I am, as you know,
an esquire. I swear to God that if I met a
count in the street and he did not salute me,
I would not salute him if I met him again.
I should enter some house as if I had business
there, or turn down another street before he
came near me. For a gentleman owes nothing
to any one but God and the king ; nor is it
right for a man of honour to forego his self-

The esquire tells his story to Lazaro.

The esquire expounds his views of honour to Lazaro.

74

respect. I remember that one day, in my country, I affronted and nearly came to blows with an officer, because whenever I saluted him he said, 'May God preserve your honour!' 'You are a wretch,' I said, 'for you are not well bred. You said to me "God preserve you," as if I was nobody.' From that time he took off his cap, and behaved properly."
"Is it not good manners for one man to salute another," I asked, "or to say 'God preserve you'?" He answered, "It is only underbred people who talk thus. To gentlemen like myself, it should be not less than 'I kiss the hands of your honour!' or at the very least, 'I kiss your hand, sir!' if he who speaks is a knight. In my own land I would not suffer a mere 'God preserve you,' nor will I suffer it from any man in the world, from The esquire continues to discourse on the same subject. the king downwards." "Sinner that I am," said I, "for having taken so little care about it. But will you not suffer any one to pray for you?"

He continued: "Above all, I am not so poor but that I possess, in my own country, an estate of houses which are well-built, sixteen leagues from where I was born, in the vicinity of Valladolid. They would be worth two hundred times a thousand maravedis if they were in good repair; and I also have a pigeon-cote which, if it was not demolished, would give out two hundred pigeons every year, as well as other things about which I am silent, as it might touch my honour.

" I came to this city because I expected to find a good appointment, but things have not turned out as I thought. Canons The esquire's and other Churchmen find plenty, honour makes him fastidious because their profession is not over-in accepting employment. crowded. Careless gentlemen also seek me, but to serve with such people involves great trouble, for a man must lose his self-respect with them. If not they tell you to go in God's name, while the pay is usually at long intervals; when they wish to clear their consciences, and pay for your work, they make you free of a wardrobe containing a worn doublet and a frayed cloak. When Service with a a man takes service with a titled great lord is not to the lord there is also misery. I cannot esquire's liking. undertake to serve or content such. By the Lord! if I should engage myself to one, I think that I should be a great favourite, and that he would confer great favours on me; but I should have to like his habits and customs though not the best in the world; I should be expected never to say a word that would displease, to be very careful in word and deed, not to kill myself in doing things

76

which the great man would not see, never to
consort with those who would do him dis-
service because it would behove me to guard
his interests. If some servant of his excites
his anger by neglecting his duties, and it
should appear that something might be said
for the accused, on the contrary you must
scoff at the poor fellow maliciously. It is a
duty to inform against those in the house, and
to find out what is done outside, so as to
report it. Many other things of a like kind
are the custom in a palace, and with the lord
of it, who appears honourable. But such
lords do not want to see virtuous men in their
houses. On the contrary, they hate and
despise them, calling them useless and un-
acquainted with business. I do not wish to
trust my fortunes with such people."

In this way my master was lamenting his
ill-fortune, and giving me an account of his
valorous person. While he was When the
thus employed a man and an old people came for
woman came in by the door. The their rent, the
esquire dis-
man asked for the rent of the house, appeared.
and the old woman for the rent of the bed,
saying that they were hired from two months
to two months. I think the sum required
was twelve to thirteen reals. My master
gave them a very civil answer, saying that

he would go out and get change, and return
in the afternoon.

But his departure was without any return.
They returned in the afternoon when it was
late, and I told them that he had not yet come
back. The night came, but he did not. I
was afraid to stay in the house alone, so
I went to my girl-friends, told them what had
happened, and slept there. When morning
came the creditors returned and asked for the
lodger. The girls answered that his boy was
there, and that the key was in the door.
They asked me where my master was, and I
answered that I did not know where he was,
but that he had gone out to get change. I
thought that he had gone with the change
from me as well as from them.

When they had heard what I had to say they
went for an officer and a scrivener. Presently
they returned with them. They
took the key, called me and some
witnesses, opened the door and went
in to take possession of my master's
effects until he had paid his debts. They
went all over the house and found it empty.
Then they asked me where my master's effects
were, his chest, clothes, and jewelry. I said
that I did not know. No doubt, they said,
they have got up in the night and taken

Creditors search for the esquire's effects, but there are none.

78

"They returned in the afternoon."

them somewhere else. " Sir," they said to the officer, " take this boy into custody, for he knows where the effects are."
Lazaro is taken into custody.
On this the officer came and took me by the collar, saying, " Boy, you are my prisoner if you do not show us the goods of your master."

I never was in such a plight as this, though I had been taken by the collar many times. I was dreadfully frightened and began to cry, promising to tell them all they might ask. " That is well," they said, " tell all you know and you have nothing to fear."

The scrivener then sat down on the bench to write out the inventory, asking me what there was. I said, " What my master has, according to what he told me, is a very good estate consisting of houses and a demolished pigeon-cote." " This is worth little," they said, " but it will do for the payment of his debts. In what part of the town is it ? " " In his own country," I replied. " By the Lord ! this is a fine business," they exclaimed, " and where is his country ? " " He told me that it was in Old Castille," I said. The officer and the scrivener laughed a good deal, and said, " This is a good story to cover your debts ! "

The girls who were my neighbours, and who were present, then said : " Sirs ! this is

an innocent child, and has only been a few
days with that esquire, and knows no more
Lazaro is than your worships. He used to
released, at the come to our house and we gave him
intercession of
his girl-friends. to eat what we could spare, for the
love of God, and at night he went to sleep
with the esquire."

Seeing that I was innocent they let me go.
Then the officer and the scrivener asked for
their fees from the man and the old woman,
over which there was much contention and
noise. They declared that they ought not to
be forced to pay, for they had got nothing to
pay with, and that the seizure of goods had
not been made. The others maintained that
they had been taken away from other business
of more consequence. Finally, after making
a great noise, they went away, and I do not
know how it ended.

Having rested from my past troubles I
went about to seek employment. Thus I
Lazaro finds left my poor third master, and know
himself de-
serted by his not his unhappy fate. Looking
master. back at all that had gone against
me, I found that I had managed my affairs
in a reverse way. Masters are usually deserted by their boys, but with me it was
not so. For my master deserted and fled
from me.

FOURTH MASTER

I HAD to seek for my fourth master. He was a friar of the Order of Mercy, who was pointed out to me by my girl-friends. They called him a relation. He was a great enemy of the choir, and of having his meals in the convent. He was fond of walking about, of secular business, and of paying visits, so much so that I think he wore out more shoes than any one else in the convent. The friar gave me the first shoes I ever burst in my life. They did not last eight days. I could not endure so much trotting about. For this reason, and some other little things I will not mention, I left him.

FIFTH MASTER

HOW LAZARO TOOK SERVICE WITH A SELLER OF PAPAL INDULGENCES

My fifth master chanced to be a man engaged in the sale of Papal Indulgences.[1] He was the most shameless and impudent distributor of them that ever I saw or hope to see, nor do I believe that any one else ever saw one like him. For he had and sought out his own modes and methods, and very cunning inventions. Coming to the place where he wanted to effect the sales, he began by making trifling presents to the clergy, but nothing of any great value: a lettuce of Murcia if it was the season, a couple of lemons or oranges, a peach, a couple of nectarines, or some green pears. In this way he got them into good humour for favouring his business, and inducing their parishioners to buy his Indulgences.

[1] The "Pardoner," or seller of Indulgences, was also caricatured in Chaucer's *Canterbury Tales*, a century and a half earlier.

LAZARILLO DE TORMES

If they said that they understood Latin, he did not say a word in that language, for fear of stumbling, but he resorted to a gentle and well-considered way of telling his story, with a most seductive tongue. If he found that the clergy were of the reverend class, he talked to them in Latin for two hours, at least what appeared like Latin, though it might not have been so. When the people did not buy the Indulgences freely, he sought how to make them do so by bringing trouble on their village. At other times he tried cunning tricks. But as all his devices would take long to relate, I will only recount one that was specially subtle, and proved his sufficiency.

He had preached for two or three days in a village near Toledo, using all his accustomed arts, but no one had bought an Indulgence, nor was there any sign of an intention to do so. He had devoted them all to the Devil, and was meditating what to do next, when he determined to call the parishioners together the next morning and make a last effort. That night he and the constable,[1] after supper,

---

[1] A pardoner always had a sergeant or constable with him, to help him in such houses as refused to pay for their pardons at the appointed time.

sat down to play at cards, and they began to
quarrel over the game, and make use of bad
Sham quarrel language. The seller of Indulgences
between the called the constable a thief, and
seller of
Indulgences and the constable called him a liar.
the constable. On this my master took up a
lance which was in the doorway. The constable put his hand on his sword. At the row
they were making the guests and neighbours
came and got between them. In great fury
the combatants struggled to free themselves
and get at each other. But as the place was
full of people they saw that they would be
prevented from fighting, so they again resorted
to abusive language. Among other things
the constable said to my master that he was a
liar, and that the Indulgences about which he
preached were false. At last the people, as
they could not pacify the disputants, determined to take the constable away. Thus my
master was left in a great rage. Later on
the guests and neighbours entreated him to
moderate his anger and go to bed, which in
the end we all did.

When morning came my master went to
the church to arrange about the Mass, and
about preaching the sermon to announce
the Indulgences. The people assembled, but
they came murmuring at the Indulgences,

saying that they were false, and that the constable himself had found it out. If before they disliked buying them they <small>The seller of</small> now detested the idea. The com- <small>Indulgences begins his</small> missary or seller of Indulgences went <small>sermon.</small> up into the pulpit, and began his sermon by urging the people not to fail in getting the benefit of such a blessing and such Indulgences as the sacred Bull brought them. When he was in the middle of his sermon the constable entered by the door of the church, and when he had said a prayer, he got up and addressed the people in a loud voice. "Good people," he said, "hear one word from me, <small>Sham</small> and then listen to any one you like. <small>denunciation of the</small> I came here with this cheat who is <small>Indulgences by</small> preaching to you, and he deceived <small>the constable.</small> me. He said that I should help him in this business, and that we would divide the profits. Now see the harm he would have done to my conscience and to your pockets. I plainly declare to you that the Indulgences he is preaching about are false, and that you should not believe in them nor buy them. I will not be a party to it, directly nor indirectly. From this time I give up the wand of office and put it on the ground. If hereafter this man is punished for his falsehoods, you must be my witness that I am not a party to them,

and have neither aided nor abetted them. On
the contrary, I have undeceived you and
exposed his imposture." Then he concluded
his speech.

Some respectable men wanted to take the
constable and turn him out of the church to
avoid scandal. But my master raised his hand
and ordered that no one should molest him on
pain of excommunication. He declared that
the constable must be allowed to say whatever
he liked. When the constable had finished,
my master asked him whether he wanted to
say anything more. The constable replied, "I
could say a good deal more about your falsehoods, but this will do for the present."

The commissary then knelt down in the
pulpit, clasped his hands, turned his eyes up,
and said : "O Lord ! from whom nothing is
hidden, and to whom all things are known, to
whom nothing is impossible but all things are
possible, Thou knowest the truth and how
unjustly I have been accused. All that con-
cerns myself I freely pardon, as Thou, Lord,
hast pardoned me. Look not at this man
who knows not what he does or says. I only
pray for justice. Some who are present may
perchance have intended to take these holy
Indulgences, and on hearing the false words of
that man they may have changed their minds.

So I pray to Thee, O Lord, that Thou wilt work a miracle in this way. If what my accuser says is true, that I am evil and false, let this pulpit sink from me forty feet under ground, and never appear again. But if what I say is true, and that man is persuaded by the Devil to try to deprive those present of such great benefits, let him be punished, that all may know his malice."

Sham miracle worked on the constable.

Scarcely had my devout master finished his speech when the bad constable fell to the ground with such a noise that the church resounded. Then he began to groan and foam at the mouth, making hideous faces, throwing about his arms and legs, and rolling about on the ground. The noise made by the people was so great that they could not hear each other speak. Some were astounded and terrified. Others cried to God for help. A few, not without trepidation, took his arms and held his legs, for there is not a mule in the world that could have given fiercer kicks. So they held him for a long time, there being more than fifteen men keeping him down, and to all he gave blows, and, if they were not careful, kicks also.

All this time my master was on his knees in the pulpit, with hands and eyes raised to heaven, transported by the divine essence.

The noise and disturbance in the church had no effect on his sacred contemplations. Some good men came to him, and, speaking loudly to arouse him, entreated him to succour that poor creature who was dying. They besought him not to dwell upon things that were past, and not to consider his evil deeds, as he had been punished. They prayed to him that, if he could do any good, he would deliver the man from his sufferings for the love of God. They declared that they clearly saw the sin of the culprit, and my master's truth and goodness, but entreated him to pray to the Lord not to prolong the man's punishment. The commissary, like one awaking from a delicious dream, looking long at the culprit and at those who were round him, then said : "My good friends, you have interceded for a man on whom God has so signally laid his Hands. But He has enjoined us not to return evil for evil, and to pardon injuries. We may confidently pray that His goodness will pardon this offender who has tried to put obstacles into the working of His holy faith. Let us all pray for this."

He then came down from the pulpit, and desired that all should pray very devoutly to our Lord to pardon that sinner, and restore him

The people intercede for the constable.

All the people pray for the constable to be forgiven.

to health and sound judgment, delivering him
from the Devil, if, for his great sin, the Evil
One had been permitted to enter into him. All
went down on their knees before the altar,
while the clergy began to chant a litany in a
low voice, coming with a cross and the holy
water, after singing over it. My master raised
his hands to heaven, and turned his eyes up
until scarcely anything could be seen
but the whites. He then commenced The farce is carried on to completion.
an address not less long than devout,
which made the people weep as they do over
a sermon on the Passion delivered by a famous
preacher. He prayed to the Lord not to
require the death of the sinner, but rather to
give his life back to one who had been led
away by the Devil, that, being convinced of
his sin unto death, he might receive pardon,
life, and health, and that he might repent
and confess. This done, he would receive the
Indulgence.

Presently the sinful constable began gradu-
ally to recover until he was himself again.
When he was well, he fell at the feet of
the commissary asking for pardon, and con-
fessing that what he had said was by order of
the Devil, to do my master harm and to be
avenged on him, but principally because the
Devil was very much annoyed at the good that

was done by the Indulgences being received.
My master pardoned him, and signs of friend-
ship were passed between them.   Then there
was such eagerness to buy the Indulgences that
scarcely a soul in the place was without one —
husbands and wives, sons 'and daughters, boys
and girls.   The news of what had happened
soon spread to the neighbouring villages, and
when we came to them it was not necessary to
preach nor even to go to church.   In ten or
twelve villages of that neighbourhood where
we were, my master sold as many thousand
Indulgences, without having to preach a single
sermon.   When he performed this
farce, I confess that I was astounded
and believed like many others.   But

Lazaro was behind the scenes.

afterwards I was a witness to the jokes and
laughter that my master and the constable had
over the business.   I knew how it had been
planned and arranged by the industry and
inventive talent of my master.   Though only
a boy I fell into thought, and said to myself,
" How many more tricks will the rogues play
on these innocent people ! "   I was nearly four
months with my fifth master, during which I
also suffered plenty of hardships.

" The news soon spread to the neighbouring villages."

SIXTH MASTER

AFTER this I took service with a master who
painted tumbrels. My duty was to grind the
colours, and here also I suffered many evil
things. Having now grown to be a fine lad,
I went into the principal church, and one of
the chaplains took me to be his servant. He
gave me charge of a donkey, four jars, and a
whip. So I began to carry water for the city.
This was the first step I ascended, to reach
a decent life. For I gave thirty maravedis
of profit to my master every day, and on
Saturdays I was allowed the profits for myself,
and everything else beyond the thirty maravedis a day. I went on so well that at the
end of four years I had put something by, and
was able to dress myself very well. I bought a
doublet of fustian, a coat with sleeves, and a
woollen cloak, as well as a sword. Shortly I

95

saw myself clothed like a respectable man.
I said to my master that he might take the
donkey, as I did not intend to follow that
occupation any longer.

SEVENTH MASTER

HOW LAZARO TOOK SERVICE WITH A CONSTABLE AND WHAT HAPPENED AFTERWARDS

HAVING taken leave of the chaplain, I entered the service of a constable, but stayed a very short time with him, for my occupation appeared to me to be dangerous, especially one night when we were attacked with stones and sticks. They treated my master badly, but they could not catch me. This business made me retire from the constable's service.

Thinking how I should live so as to find some rest and save a little for my old age, it pleased God to enlighten me, and to put me on a profitable road. With the favour of friends and patrons all my labours and hardships, up to that time, were repaid, on reaching what I sought and obtained. This was a Government appointment such as enabled no one to thrive except those who occupied it. In it I live and reside to this day, in the service of God and your Honour.

LAZARILLO DE TORMES

My duty is to have charge of the inspection of wine that is sold in this city, as well at Lazaro gets public sales as elsewhere, also to a Government appointment, accompany those who are condemned and is married. for default, and to cry out their transgressions, being a crier speaking in good Castillian. It has happened also that almost everything appertaining to the office passes through my hands, throughout the whole city. He who wants to draw wine for sale may reckon on deriving little profit, unless Lazaro de Tormes is consulted in the matter.

At this time his Honour the Archpriest of St. Saviour's,[1] my lord and the friend of your worship, seeing my cleverness and noticing my presentable appearance when employed by him in announcing his wines, made an arrangement that I should marry one of his servant girls. Seeing myself that this would bring me benefits and favours, I gave my consent. I was married to her, and to this day I have had no reason to repent it, for I

[1] Formerly there were two kinds of parishes in Toledo. Those of the *Muzarabes*, founded by the Gothic King Athanagild, the grandfather of St. Ildefonso, continued through Moorish times. They were existing when Alfonso VI. took Toledo in 1085. Their number was six, reduced to two. The others were called *Latinas*, formed afterwards, of which there were twenty reduced to nine. St. Saviour's was one of the latter. It has been joined to that of San Pedro since Lazarillo's time.

found her to be a good girl and diligent in service. I have favour and help from my lord the Archpriest. He always gives us during the year a load of wheat, meat on festivals, sometimes loaves of fine bread, and the shoes he has left off wearing. He arranged for us to rent a small house near his own. On almost every Sunday and on feast days we dine in his house.

But evil tongues are never wanting, and never let people live in peace. They said I know not what about my wife, because she went to make the bed and cook the dinner, and in this they spoke the truth, but she was not a woman who would give occasion for their scoffing. My lord the Archpriest had promised what I think he will perform, and one day he spoke to me fully on the subject. "Lazaro de Tormes," he said, "he who listens to evil tongues will never prosper. I say this because your wife may be seen entering my house and leaving it. She comes with honour to herself and to you, and this I promise you. Do not attend to what they say, and be assured that what I tell you is for your good." I replied that I was determined to care for and preserve my honesty. "It is true," I said, "that some of my friends have spoken to me

Evil tongues.

about this, and have even certified to me that before I was married to my wife she had borne a child three times, speaking with reverence to your Worship." My wife took such oaths on the subject that I thought the house would come down upon us, and then she began to weep and to curse the day she had married me. She went on in such a way that I wished I had died before I let such words out of my mouth.

I on one side and the Archpriest on the other entreated her to leave off crying, and I swore that never in all my life would I refer to the matter again. I declared that I should rejoice to see her go in and out of our patron's house whenever she liked, as I was convinced A good of her honesty. So we all three understanding. continued to have a good understanding as to this, and have never heard more about it. When any one tries to say anything I stop him by saying: "Look here! if you are a friend do not say anything that will annoy me, for I do not look upon him as my friend who causes me sorrow, more especially if he tries to make trouble between me and my wife, for she is the thing in the world that I care for most. I love her, and may God show favour to her. She is a far better wife than I deserve, and I swear before the con-

" But evil tongues are never wanting."

secrated host that she is as good a woman
as can be found within the gates of Toledo.
He who says the contrary shall answer to me
for it." By this means I manage that they
shall say nothing, and I have peace in my
house.

This was in the same year that our vic-
torious Emperor entered into this famous city
of Toledo, and held the Cortes here,[1]

Conclusion.

and there were great rejoicings
as your Worship will have heard. At this
time I was prosperous and at the summit of all
good fortune.

PRINTED AT BURGOS IN THE HOUSE OF JUAN
DE JUNTA IN THE YEAR 1554

[1] In 1525, at the time when Francis I. arrived as a prisoner
at Madrid, Charles held a General Cortes of Castille at Toledo.
There were present most of the Grandees, and all the foreign
Ambassadors. The Viceroy Carlos de Lannoy arrived at Toledo,
and was cordially received by the Emperor, after having brought
Francis to Madrid. The Cortes petitioned Charles to marry
Isabel, the Infanta of Portugal ; while the English Ambassadors
proposed to him his cousin, Mary Tudor. The Cortes sat until
the end of August.—*Sandoval*, i. 664 (2).

Sketch Map of the Route
from
SALAMANCA
to
TOLEDO

Route marked thus ············

Accompanying 'The Life of Lazarillo de Tormes.' Translated by Sir Clements R. Markham, K.C.B. (A. & C. Black.)

LEDESMA

R. Tormes

SALAMANCA
Calvarasa
Tejares
Alba de Tormes

BEJAR

Piedrahita

Horcajo

Sierra de Gredos

ARENAS

Mijares

Navamorcuendo

Cervera

Navalacruz

Puerto del Pico

AVILA

S. Martin de Val de iglesia

Almorox

ESCALONA

Magueda

Torrijos

TOLEDO
Aroes
Layos
Polan
Galvez
Pulgar

La Puebla

TALAVERA

Alberche R.

R. Tagus

BORDER of PORTUGAL

INDEX

PEOPLE MENTIONED

PLACES MENTIONED

INDEX

VICTUALS AND DRINK MENTIONED BY LAZARO

Note—But only those with * eaten or drunk by Lazaro. The rest only talked about.

CPSIA information can be obtained at www.ICGtesting.com
Printed in the USA
LVOW120748130613

338389LV00001B/186/P